School for UNUSUAL MAGIC

THE EQUINOX TEST

WRITTEN AND ILLUSTRATED BY

LIZ MONTAGUE

SCHOLASTIC PRESS
NEW YORK

Library of Congress Cataloging-in-Publication Data
Names: Montague, Liz, author, illustrator.
Title: The equinox test / Liz Montague.
Description: New York : Scholastic Press, 2024. | Series: School for unusual magic ; 1 | Audience: Ages 8–12. | Audience: Grades 4–6. | Summary: Rose, Amethyst, and Lavender, fifth-year students at the Brooklyn School of Magic, need to pass the Equinox Test in order to move up to Middle Magic—but they soon face self-doubts, a cheating scandal, and trouble brewing in the magical community.
Identifiers: LCCN 2023025428 (print) | LCCN 2023025429 (ebook) | ISBN 9781338792515 | ISBN 9781338792522 (ebook)
Subjects: LCSH: Magic—Juvenile fiction. | Students—Juvenile fiction. | Schools—Juvenile fiction. | Self-confidence—Juvenile fiction. | Cheating (Education)—Juvenile fiction. | Friendship—Juvenile fiction. | Brooklyn (New York, N.Y.)—Juvenile fiction. | CYAC: Magic—Fiction. | Students—Fiction. | Schools—Fiction. | Self-confidence—Fiction. | Cheating—Fiction. | Friendship—Fiction. | Brooklyn (New York, N.Y.)—Fiction. | BISAC: JUVENILE FICTION / Fantasy & Magic | JUVENILE FICTION / Action & Adventure / General | LCGFT: Fantasy fiction. | Novels.
Classification: LCC PZ7.1.M6436 Eq 2024 (print) | LCC PZ7.1.M6436 (ebook) | DDC 813.6 [Fic]—dc23/eng/20230530
LC record available at https://lccn.loc.gov/2023025428
LC ebook record available at https://lccn.loc.gov/2023025429

10 9 8 7 6 5 4 3 2 1   24 25 26 27 28

Printed in Italy 183
First edition, April 2024
Book design by Omou Barry

To Brooklyn and Chatham—thank you for sharing your magic

Chapter 1
ROSE

Rose Vera was certain an army of ants marched under her skin.

That must be the reason she felt nerves coursing through her body—it was their tiny feet. Her hands shook as she opened her school's door, further proof of the ant army's movement. The stress couldn't possibly be coming from Rose herself or have anything to do with the meeting she was about to have with the principal. Ants were *much* more believable.

Onward! Get those tiny feet moving!

Rose lingered, one foot planted on the Brooklyn sidewalk, the other resting on marble floors. It was a bad habit. Doors were for going in or out, not waffling in between. But she couldn't help it today. Not when the silhouette of her parents was getting smaller and smaller as they disappeared down the hallway ahead of her.

They hadn't waited for her. Rose knew she'd very colorfully demanded they go on without her just a few minutes earlier, but still, now she was nervous . . . and alone.

The door started to feel heavy against her hand. Rose gave it a shove and found that the normally cooperative door was refusing to move.

Typical. But then, this *was* the Brooklyn School of Magic. There was never a guarantee things would stay normal. From the outside the decayed wooden door of the old brownstone was barely holding on to its hinges, decorated only by the occasional spider. But on the inside it was elegant glass, the rest of Brooklyn on display through its frosted panes.

"Traitor!" Rose grumbled, leaning her full weight into it, her flip-flops beginning to slide under the pressure. "Nothing is on my side today," she declared with one last shove as the door clicked shut.

It was barely morning and Rose had already endured two betrayals: First, their annual end-of-summer Coney Island trip, which was just days away, had been canceled for no good reason. Rose remembered her mom mentioning something about unsafe tides, but weren't tides and water kind of the whole point of the ocean? Second, her parents had actually listened to her for once and left her abandoned in the hallway battling the door all alone.

She forced her legs to move. The Brooklyn School of Magic had always reminded Rose of a glass castle, complete with its very own river that twisted through the halls. The school seemed too delicate for the weathered buildings that surrounded it. Well, sort of surrounded it. The campus was at least a few hundred acres, though no one could tell from the outside. Rose wasn't sure how that worked. Her classmate Chamomile Mills claimed she'd once stumbled onto a mountain range that could only be accessed through a secret door at the back of the gymnasium. Not that Rose trusted Chamomile Mills for one second.

As she walked to the principal's office, Rose was surprised so many students were here on a Saturday morning. She'd been forced to come and had scowled the entire four-block walk here past Fort Greene Park and up DeKalb Avenue. But her classmates, smiling and laughing among the flowers in the school's Meadowlark Courtyard, had no excuse.

These were the last days of summer and here they were, wasting it at school.

Granted, Rose was a day student—she came in the mornings and went home every afternoon. But plenty of students boarded at the school, and it seemed some had arrived a few weeks before the school year was set to begin. Students like Amethyst Vern, Rose's best friend. Rose tried to spot Amethyst reading in front of one of the cozy tree houses that sat at the far side of the courtyard, although, knowing Amethyst, she was probably in her room color-coding tea leaves or getting a head start on all the homework they'd have to do in their fifth-year classes. All Elementary Magic boarders lived in the middle levels of the tree dorms, but next year, when they moved up to Middle Magic, Amethyst would get a room high in the leafy green canopy.

Middle Magic. Just the thought made Rose's heart stutter.

Swallowing down the burning in her chest, she waved to Jasmine Ward and Magnolia Bartlett, then shielded her eyes from the ruthless sun. It beamed through a massive skylight that stretched the length of the courtyard. From what Rose could make out, Jasmine and Magnolia were huddled on a patch of grass soaking in the rays. Jasmine seemed to be charming a daisy petal, her eyes closed and her lips muttering softly as the petal on her palm swelled to the size of a pillow.

That was a popular spell from their fourth-year Enchantments class. Daisy petals were perfect to lean against or rest on when chatting with friends, not to mention soft as silk. Plus, the daisies never seemed to mind. They had so many petals that taking one here and there wasn't damaging—not like plucking one from an orchid, which would put up a real fuss.

Jasmine gave Rose a warm smile and a wave, but Magnolia only offered a half-hearted grimace. Magnolia had been in Rose's Botany class last year and must have remembered her outburst—Rose had almost failed the class because of it. They'd been doing dissections for a lesson on flower arrangements, which Rose had said looked like a crime scene. Picking a flower killed it. But Ms. Blossom, the head gardener who taught Botany, had not been pleased to be accused of plant murder.

More than once Rose wished she could be like Amethyst, able to give school her full attention and care. To not say every thought that popped into her mind. It was because of Amethyst that Rose understood the basics of Elementary Magic at all: easy spells to change the makeup of things,

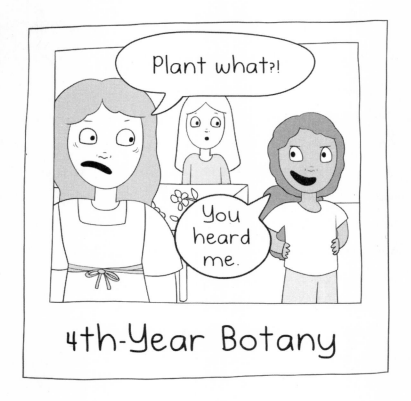

charms that manipulated appearance, and potions that affected thoughts and feelings. Still, Rose struggled to keep it all straight sometimes, using spells to charm and charms to spell.

But even if the "school" part of school wasn't entirely her thing, Rose loved being part of this community. The magic of stumbling across a door that took you, allegedly, to a mountain range; thousand-year-old trees that could be home to ten-year-old students; and daisies that offered up their petals like people gave smiles at the corner store. Those were the moments Rose didn't want to lose. She just couldn't.

Because even before Rose arrived at the principal's office, before she heard the hushed tones of her parents talking or saw Principal Ivy look up at her with a concerned smile, Rose knew what this Saturday meeting was about. She could feel it. Her outburst in Ms. Blossom's class hadn't been the only time she'd gotten in trouble during the past four years. And, despite Amethyst's best efforts, Rose was barely keeping up in class.

So as much as she wanted to remain part of the Brooklyn School of Magic, Rose wasn't sure the Brooklyn School of Magic wanted her back.

Chapter 2
ROSE

Rose's heart had stopped once before. She'd been walking across the beams in her attic ceiling after seeing one of the neighborhood cats, Jax, swish along the wooden planks. Jax was very social and adventurous, the total opposite of his brother, Felix, who mainly stayed hidden at the school. But Rose wasn't Felix or Jax—she'd nearly fallen off the beam, her heart freezing until she found her footing again.

As Principal Ivy spoke, Rose's heart stopped again. This time was different, like all of Brooklyn had frozen in time. But if that were true, the words coming out of her principal's mouth would stop, and Rose wouldn't have to hear that everything was about to change. Rose looked down at her lap, the thrumming in her chest sounding newer and louder.

"Transferring schools isn't a bad thing," Principal Ivy was saying. "Right now, we're just considering the possibility. We just want you to be somewhere that's a good fit."

"I don't fit in here?" Rose kept her voice low, trying to shove her tears back into her eyes.

Sure, her brews could've been more potent, and maybe her gardens were always last to bud, but she was still learning. She had time to get her Magic Bearing skills to where her classmates' were. Didn't she?

"Different pupils need different things." Principal Ivy tented her fingers, looking earnestly in Rose's direction. "As we consider your future, we just want you to be in an environment where you can succeed." Principal Ivy pushed a pamphlet toward her. ROGERS MIDDLE SCHOOL was printed across the top in bold yellow letters, and smiling students dotted the cover. Rose didn't pick it up. She'd walked past Rogers Middle nearly every day of her life. What more information could she need? Rose even knew a few kids who went there. But none of them were Magic Bearers.

Rose's parents, who sandwiched her on either side, nodded their heads encouragingly. Once, when Rose was only in her first year of Elementary Magic, her mom and dad had considered holding her back so she'd have more time to learn the material. She'd never be a superstar at spells the way her older brother, Reed, was, but she'd proved to her parents that she could keep up, that she was good enough. Or at least, she'd thought she had.

Embarrassment started to bubble inside Rose. Everyone

passed on to Middle Magic. *Everyone.* Middle Magic went beyond the color spells, size charms, and simple herbal potions—which, in Rose's opinion, were just fancy tea—that had made up the last four years of Rose's Elementary Magic education. The fifth and final year of Elementary Magic wasn't even anything new really, just polishing up style and technique.

Middle Magic was where life truly began—it was where Magic Bearers began to cast more complex spells, where they learned things like Levitation, Invisibility, and even Shifting.

"I want to succeed here," Rose insisted.

Principal Ivy must have seen the panic dawning in Rose's eyes like a sunrise. "This isn't a final decision, just something that's on the table. None of us want you to be surprised should an adjustment need to be made." She gave Rose an encouraging smile. "We're all on your side, Rose."

No, you're not, Rose thought as her mother and father continued to nod.

"We just want what's best for you."

No, you don't. Rose bit her lip. She would fight this. She would show them all just how wrong they were about her.

Chapter 3
LAV

Lav Barros had made the long trek from the subway to the Brooklyn School of Magic many times before. The first time, three years ago, he'd only come up to his father's elbow, his head swiveling constantly trying to follow all the honking cars on the busy road. They were so different from the Vespas and bicycles he'd grown up with on Île Violette, a speck of an island—maybe a half speck—near the coast of France. Lost in the busyness of the street, he almost hadn't realized that he and his dad had reached their destination: a crumbling brownstone that looked practically abandoned.

"This," his father had said, a proud smile growing on his lips as he raised his arms wide, taking it all in, "is why we've come to America."

This? Lav thought as the shattered windows stared at him, ominous and vacant. He'd only been eight at the time and hadn't fully realized yet that they wouldn't be returning to Île Violette's familiar sun and sands and sea, to his grandmother's songs or the white house on the hill that he'd called home his entire life. But Lav understood enough to know that, whatever they'd moved to New York for, it could not be for the wreck standing before them.

No, his parents must've had a better reason to leave paradise. That's what Lav reminded himself on the days when their cramped apartment felt suffocating and the endless sirens on their street were especially ear-shattering. The weeks they'd spent visiting his dad's friend over the summer in Chicago had proved it wasn't just New York—everywhere was too loud and too crowded. Everywhere but home.

For generations, Île Violette had been his family's whole world. But the water surrounding the island had started getting rougher. Waves as tall as mountains crept closer and closer to the shore as the water seemed to battle under the surface. The day Lav's family left the island, the waves had crashed only a block away from their front door. Lav knew his parents must have truly been at their limit to think starting over in a place like this was a good idea. But they were just waiting for things to cool down back home, Lav was sure of it. Brooklyn was just for now, not forever.

And so was the rickety-looking school his parents had chosen for him.

"Are you sure?" Lav had asked his father, the unfamiliar English words thick in his mouth. "Do you have the right address?"

"First impressions can be deceiving. Look again," his dad had said, beaming like the morning sun.

Lav turned back to the abandoned brownstone. The facade had melted like sand falling through fingers. One moment there were boarded-up windows and loose bricks, the next sleek glass windows and smooth stone archways had planted themselves in full view. The building resembled a cathedral-sized greenhouse, all sunlight and airy spaces. It was larger than made sense for the bustling street corner on DeKalb Avenue and St. James Place.

It's a bit much, Lav had thought. Back home on Île Violette, he'd just taken lessons with his grandmother. She'd give him sweets and tell stories about all she'd seen and done in her life. During their last lesson, when he'd had to say goodbye, she'd wiped the tears streaming from his eyes. "I'll teach you how to come back," she'd promised. "Home will always be part of you."

He'd taken her up on that promise many times over the last three years.

But today, Lav was alone. And while autumn teased its arrival, the first day of class was still a few weeks away. He was on a mission.

The front door's hinges creaked as Lav stepped into the school. He considered himself someone who made good choices. Mostly. Usually. But as he rushed through the halls, he hoped his plan was one of them. Today wasn't even the day he'd put the plan into action. He was just at school to gather information.

His parents were at work, and he had a few hours before he'd promised to meet his grandma, so he'd come to make sure he knew his way around the Specialty Magic wing. Elementary students never came to this side of the school. But he needed to know where the Correspondence Room was. The last thing Lav wanted was to ruin everything because he'd gotten lost when it mattered.

Lav was an okay student. Not bad, not great—just solidly average. His grades were far below what they should be, given everything it had cost his family to get him here. He always felt behind the other kids. But not this year. During that visit to Chicago, he'd gotten the nudge he'd needed to finally make things a little more fair. If his plan turned out how he hoped, maybe acing his classes would prove to his parents that it was time for them to move back home, that he'd learned all the school had to teach him and he could leave with his head held high.

As Lav approached the Meadowlark Courtyard, he slowed his pace, not wanting to look too in a hurry.

"Hey, Lavender!" some of his classmates shouted as he

walked. Hugo Lilt was waving especially eagerly, a broad smile the size of a basketball floating where his head should be. *A magnifying charm no doubt*, Lav thought. Hugo was a nice guy, but he could sometimes be a show-off.

Lav waved in what he hoped was a casual manner but didn't stop walking. He'd catch up with Hugo and the other boys in his class once school started. Lav noticed a few of them smirking and pointing at him. He tried to ignore the singsong way they called his full name as he crossed the courtyard and headed down the hall.

Tired of the snickers, he'd started going by "Lav" after his first year in Elementary Magic, the same year he'd tried to lose his accent by saying the word "hamburger" in the mirror until his jaw hurt. Lavender grew everywhere on Île Violette, and when he was small, the name had felt like a piece of home. But he wasn't in his fishing village anymore.

This was Brooklyn. And Lav Barros was not anyone to laugh at.

Chapter 4
ROSE

"Amethyst probably needs help unpacking." Rose didn't look up from the floor as she mumbled to her parents. Her face was puffy and her espresso-colored eyes felt raw. "Can I go help her?"

Rose had been set free of the principal's office, but the shadow of their conversation still hung over her. Facing the threat of Rogers Middle and the impossible mountain of Middle Magic was, officially, a Difficult Problem. And the only person Rose trusted with Difficult Problems was Amethyst Vern.

"Yes, you can go help Amethyst, but—"

Rose had already started walking slowly backward toward the end of the hall as her mom spoke. She wasn't ready to hear any "buts"—she'd been through enough already that day.

"But we're going to talk more about this when you get home!" Rose's mom finished.

Rose flashed her parents a thumbs-up and turned around

the corner and out of sight. She walked past the second-grade classroom where she'd cast her very first spell—a light breeze she'd accidentally summoned for the wind chime in the window. Only it wouldn't stop ringing, and her Horticulture teacher, Mr. Fleur, had not been pleased by the interruption.

Rose traveled down a corridor full of cubbies for day students, and over the footbridge across the river. The clear blue water circled the entire ground-floor perimeter and was home to countless creatures. She tried to spot her favorite koi fish, Kyle, but was in too much of a hurry to stop and gossip about what he'd heard in the Under City. Rose cut through the Eastern Garden, which grew food for the cafeteria, raced up a back staircase, and finally arrived at the door to the rooftop courtyard she knew Amethyst loved.

Rose spotted her friend curled up with a book in the shadow of a large tree. Rose slipped off her flip-flops and walked barefoot across the moss-covered ground. She savored the furry feeling that tickled her feet as she made her way to the giant redwood tree at the center of the courtyard. It was six hundred feet high and as thick as a football field—a massive wooden skyscraper.

"This is the worst day of my life," Rose said in greeting.

"But it's not even noon." Amethyst stood, worry coloring her face as she took in Rose's tearstained cheeks. She tucked a lock of onyx hair behind her ear and adjusted her ruby-red glasses, which twinkled in the sunlight. "Tell me everything."

Rose filled Amethyst in on what Principal Ivy said as they walked to her room.

"I can't believe she doubted you like that," Amethyst sympathized.

"Right! You've seen me try in class a thousand times. I focus my mind on the spells, just like I'm supposed to. I try to connect to my 'inner force' and become one with whatever pine cone or flower seed I'm holding and . . . nothing." Frustration bubbled inside Rose. "It's not my fault. Maybe I don't have an inner pine cone. Has anyone ever considered that? And maybe that's not a bad thing since, last time I checked, I'm not a tree!"

Amethyst squinted through her glasses. "Well, technically we're supposed to be one with everything, at least a little bit. It's kind of how our magic works."

"Congratulations. You've cracked the code." Rose hung an imaginary medal around Amethyst's neck. "That's why my magic doesn't work how it's supposed to—I'm one with nothing." Rose sighed dramatically. "I'm a single sock, lost in the dryer. A lone ranger, like Jax." Rose's eyebrows shot up. "There's a thought. I could roam the neighborhood, run totally wild. Jax has a great life and he didn't make it to Middle Magic either."

"Jax is a cat, Rose." It was the look of true concern in Amethyst's eyes as she spoke that made Rose break into a fit of giggles.

"You're better at spells than I am," complimented Rose. "Turn me into a cat. Better yet, make it a charm, so I just *seem* like a cat, but really I'm still me."

"I'll pass, thank you," Amethyst responded.

"Oh, come on." Rose crossed her arms. "If you wanted to be a cat, I'd turn you into one. I'd even make you little cat glasses."

Amethyst rolled her eyes. "Cats rely more on their sense of smell and hearing than their vision. If I was a cat, I wouldn't even need glasses."

"So you'll consider it?" Rose's grin grew.

Amethyst took a deep breath. "I can't turn you into a cat without major help from a huge power source. Like a wand, which are highly illegal. That much concentrated power puts all of us in danger. Wands sap our magic like parasites. Plus, cutting a wand kills the tree the wand was cut from, and thus that tree no longer feeds energy into the earth—or the magic Nature's given us—which could be really bad for all Magic Bearers. And most importantly, if I was found in possession of a wand, I would get in big trouble. Nature could decide to take away my magic altogether. But for you, my best friend, if you *really* needed me to, I would find a way to turn you into a cat."

From the look in her eyes, Rose knew Amethyst meant it. And Rose knew how lucky she was to have a friend who made big promises and kept them.

She pondered deeply for a second before responding, "Did you really just say 'thus'?"

Shaking her head, Amethyst smiled and pressed a knot in the tree bark of Redwood Dorm. An elevator-sized door in the trunk slipped open, and the girls stepped inside. She pushed the button for the middle bark, where the ten- and eleven-year-old boarders' dorm rooms were.

Last year Amethyst's dorm room had been in the tangled roots downstairs. Rose hoped her new room felt just as cozy. She was certain that the best place to tackle her Difficult Problem was somewhere comfortable with someone who, no matter what, would find a way to turn you into a cat.

Chapter 5
LAV

On the other side of town, Lav was thinking about wands, too. But only because everything else in his life felt so dull. With the afternoon sun pounding mercilessly through the window of the apartment, Lav realized he'd reached a new level of boredom and flopped on the couch. He glanced at the clock, willing the minute hand to hurry up. His parents wouldn't be back from work for a few more hours, and now that his recon at school was done, he had places to go before they got home. But not for another twenty minutes.

No one, ever, in the history of existence, had been as bored as he was now. Lav used to think having magic meant he'd never be bored again. He'd pictured himself spilling over with power. He'd wave a wand and sparkles would rain down, a rainbow would sprout from the sky, and children would cheer for him in the streets.

But that wasn't how it worked—not even a little bit.

Sighing, he trudged to the kitchen and grabbed the

orange juice, chugging it straight from the carton. *No use dirtying a glass*, he thought as he smacked his lips appreciatively.

He should've known better than to think that magic would make him all-powerful. Lav's grandmother and both his parents were Magic Bearers, and he'd grown up seeing them live and work like regular people. Well, except for the occasional laundry spell here and there.

Only he'd watched too many movies. The first time his dad caught Lav waving around a loose stick from the yard and shouting made-up spells, his father's face had drained of color and he'd snatched it from Lav's hand.

His dad hadn't been angry, just frightened. He'd explained to Lav that wands were incredibly rare and dangerous. The only way to get one was to break a branch from an ancient tree whose whereabouts were kept secret. By removing the branch, the entire tree—and possibly even the whole forest—could die. Personal power wasn't worth that kind of risk.

"I can understand how it looks like we simply *have* magic," Mr. Barros had said gently. "But Magic Bearers can't just wield power without consequence. We carry magic. And carrying something this precious comes with great responsibility." Mr. Barros tossed the stick over their fence. "It's something Nature can take back."

Lav had looked glumly in the direction of his lost stick.

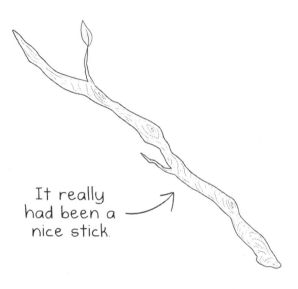

It really had been a nice stick.

He laughed to himself now just thinking about it and migrated back to the couch, kicking his feet up on the coffee table as he sank into the cushions. Just outside the window, a train screeched by, making the whole floor vibrate softly.

As the minutes ticked by, he stared at his hand. He considered it a design flaw that his fingers didn't glow or shoot purple sparks. Maybe that was something they taught in Middle Magic. But Nature knew when some-one wasn't cut out to be a Magic Bearer. It guarded its gifts. He couldn't fake having it any more than he could shake it off forever. And the worse he did in his classes, the more stuck in the middle he felt—not good enough to carry magic properly, but just magical enough to never feel like a regular kid.

Lav glanced at the clock. *Finally*, he sighed. He'd had enough of his own thoughts for today. It was time to go meet her. He saluted the empty room around him in fare-well. Boredom would have to be conquered once and for all another day.

He leaned his head back against the couch and centered his breathing from his stomach, just like his grandmother taught him.

Sometimes magic wasn't so bad, he thought as he closed his eyes. The lull of the train faded away.

Lav smiled as something inside him shifted, and the soft crashing of waves filled his ears.

Chapter 6
AMETHYST

The wooden walls of Amethyst's room were rounded like the inside of an egg and were spotted with small circular windows. Amethyst's suitcase and duffel bag were settled in the middle of the floor. Rose walked soundlessly to Amethyst's bed and collapsed onto it, face-first.

"What am I going to do?" Rose said, her voice muffled as she spoke into Amethyst's pillow.

"Just do your best, it's all you can do—" Amethyst began. She would never tell Rose this, but she could understand where Principal Ivy was coming from. Not that she wanted her friend sent away to another school—the mere thought filled Amethyst with a jolt of pure panic. But she wanted Rose to succeed and be happy—even if that meant succeeding and being happy at Rogers Middle.

"I was already doing my best," Rose snapped, lifting her head. Amethyst's hurt must have shown on her face because Rose's voice softened. "I'm sorry, I've made it all about me and haven't even asked how your move-in was."

Amethyst smiled quietly to herself at this small recognition. "Personal growth," her mother would call it.

"It's okay, you've got big news." Amethyst settled herself on the floor beside her open suitcase. Seeing her seaweed-green luggage, scuffed and covered in stickers, reminded Amethyst of the day her mom gave it to her, shiny and new for her first year boarding at school.

Originally, Amethyst and her two younger sisters, Julie and Sage, had been day students like Rose. But, two years ago, her mom had been relocated to New Jersey for a promotion at her job. That had changed everything.

Amethyst's mom had a very important job, though even before the move, Amethyst had only loosely understood what she actually did. Something sort of political? Like a diplomat or a negotiator, Amethyst thought. Although she asked a lot of questions, her mom was always pretty vague about it.

"A big part of my job at the Firm," her mom said the day she gave them the suitcases, "is maintaining communication with the Merfolk in the Under City. Land Walkers like us aren't always welcome there. But someone has to keep the peace, and because of my job, that someone is me."

Amethyst pictured her mom in elaborate scuba gear,

swimming to meetings and stowing away important information in her vast mental library. Information that made the magical world aboveground safer for everyone. Secretly, Amethyst hoped to work at the Firm one day, too. Just like her mom.

"Is it hard to keep the peace?" Amethyst had asked, not liking the thought of her mom being in dangerous situations. She held the business card her mom handed her delicately, outlining the small hummingbird in the corner.

"No, not usually." Her mom had said it casually, but that "usually" snagged Amethyst's attention. "Nature generously gives us everything we need to live above land just like Nature gives the Merfolk everything they need below land. We sometimes disagree on the best way to use those gifts or the power that comes along with them. So we try to keep things equal, maintain Nature's balance." Her mom's tight-lipped smile ended the discussion, but Amethyst still had questions.

The Under City was a mystery to her. Far below the New York Harbor, it stretched along the ocean floor, winding beneath the Hudson and East Rivers. The Merfolk's territory was full of as much history and magic and life as they had on land, though most of what Amethyst knew about their culture came from books. She'd never been to the Under City, and none of the Merfolk ever left the water.

Even Mr. Kneely, a merman who'd taught her first-year Charms class, always stayed in the river that ran through campus. He'd conducted lessons from a giant pool that took up nearly an entire floor of the Elementary wing. Her class had sat cross-legged on soft cushions around the pool while Mr. Kneely did demonstrations, using energy from the river's current to power the spells. That wasn't a skill Amethyst had ever been able to master.

And the few times Amethyst had mer-classmates, though they were river-bound, their homework had somehow always stayed dry. Amethyst may have been one of the best

students in her year, but she didn't always understand their magic, and they didn't always understand hers.

Keeping the peace between their two worlds was a big job, one that meant a lot to her mom. The least she and her sisters could do was be supportive of it—even if that meant living in New Jersey. Plus, the three girls saw their mom most weekends when she would stop by for breakfast or lunch. But that didn't make moving away at the beginning of each term any easier.

"The move-in was fine." Amethyst bit her lip anxiously. "My mom told me she's already cleared her schedule for the Blossom Ceremony." An annual tradition just before winter break, the Blossom Award was given to the most gifted student in all of Elementary Magic. It was a huge honor, second only to the Medal of Excellence in Magical Achievement, but no one ever won that so Amethyst figured it didn't count. Blossom recipients always went on to do great things in the world. Amethyst, one of the brightest in her year by far, had set her sights on it early. But now, knowing her mom not only expected her to win but had planned on it, Amethyst could feel her heart racing just thinking about it.

"My mom did a transport spell for us, thankfully. Julie brought so much stuff it would've been a nightmare to lug it all on the subway. She acts like we're leaving forever every time the school year starts." Amethyst gave a small laugh as she transferred neatly folded clothes from her suitcase to the waiting open dresser drawers. "And, of course, Sage only packed her teddy bear and a pair of pajamas. I'm shocked my mom didn't notice. But she did make sure to tell me to be careful of the school river four times. I don't know why she has such a fear of me falling into it. Nobody ever does."

"Parents worry," Rose reasoned, which was unlike her.

Amethyst knit her eyebrows as she responded, "Well, my mom worries about the wrong things."

She was proud that her mother was an important woman who did important work. But still, some days she wished that her mom could visit more often. That the Under City didn't need a peacekeeper anymore. And that her mom could move them back to Brooklyn so she and Rose could walk side by side to school like they used to. Maybe this would be the year she got everything she wanted, Blossom Award included.

Amethyst shut her now empty seaweed-green suitcase and pushed it under her bed.

Chapter 7
LAV

The air moved around Lav like a wind tunnel. He was used to the sensation by now, and even as he heard the ocean grow closer, he stayed focused. He pictured the smooth white walls of his home in Île Violette, the way seagulls perched on the flat roof and light bounced off their white feathers.

Beneath him, the lumpy softness of the couch melted into firm sand. He sank his toes in deep, small shells tickling his skin as he opened his eyes.

He was home. Sort of.

Distantly, he could still hear the honking of cars and the clatter of trains. While his body was still in New York, sitting on the couch in his sun-drenched apartment, his mind was on the island.

The shoreline was a little blurry and the salt air wafting around him felt like thin smoke. But if the only taste of home he could get had to feel like a dream, at least it was a dream he got to share.

Lav turned and faced his grandmother. She looked the

same as she always did, her black-gray hair in a bun and her loose white dress billowing in the ocean breeze.

"I've been waiting all day for this." Lav smiled and leaned into her, savoring the warmth of her shoulder. "Time wasn't moving fast enough."

"I told you not to do that!" his grandmother scolded. But she smiled as she wrapped an arm around him. "That's why we have these designated times. So you don't have to worry about when you'll see me next. I want you to be out there living, not wishing you were asleep."

"If I was asleep, could I do this?" Lav challenged, flexing his fingers and waving his arms around.

But still, he knew what she meant.

Shifting was advanced magic that sent the mind traveling away from the body. It could be very dangerous. But when his grandmother had seen the desperation on his face the day he found out he was leaving the island, she'd thought it was worth the risk. She'd taught him slowly, during the weeks of packing and saying goodbye to friends and neighbors. And daydreaming had always come naturally to Lav. Shifting was just a more focused version of that.

"How are you?" his grandmother asked as she turned to get a good look at him.

Lav was silent for a moment, unsure of how honest to be. "I'm okay, I guess," he said, his fingers carving patterns in the sand.

"What's wrong?"

"Nothing's *wrong*, it's just . . ." Lav met his grandmother's eyes. "I think I know how I can come back home for real. Not just Shifting. If I do well enough in school this year, maybe—"

"Lavender Henri Barros." He groaned at his grandmother's use of his full name. "You need to trust your parents, not scheme your way back here."

She often said this, yet Lav knew if he showed up on his grandmother's doorstep, she wouldn't turn him away. But would she send him back?

He noticed the way she looked warily out at the water. The waves were calm today, lapping lazily at the shore. He hoped that was the case in the real Île Violette, too.

"It's just . . . I'm never going to understand the way things are done at my school." Lav sighed. "Not the way the other kids do."

His grandmother gave him a squeeze. "You're doing your best, and that's more than enough. Sure, maybe they know some things you don't, but *you* know some things they don't, too."

Lav gave her a sad smile. "All I know is the ocean and that's not very helpful in Brooklyn."

"You never know." She shrugged. Her eyes looked sadder than usual.

These meetings took a lot out of her. Finding someone with your mind could be tiring, and each time they met, his grandma only seemed to half listen. Today, her seafoam-colored eyes looked hazy, her usually tight bun askew.

"How are you? How's everything back home?" Lav felt himself relax in his grandmother's presence as she began to tell him stories of the market and her garden, town gossip sprinkled in between.

He knew that she only talked about the good things with him, that she wanted the island in his mind to always be this safe and tranquil place. Lav let himself believe the picture she painted as the ocean waves hissed and the smell of lavender wafted by.

Chapter 8
ROSE

"I'm worried about this year," Rose said as she turned to lie on her back and look at the ceiling. This Difficult Problem wasn't going to solve itself, no matter how much Rose wanted it to.

"Well, then, let's make a plan." Amethyst rifled around in her backpack and produced a fresh composition book, new and ready for the school year. She turned to a crisp page and wrote in neat letters *5th Year Success*. Then she underlined it. Twice.

Rose stared at her for a long minute, torn between rolling her eyes and playing along. Amethyst had always been an overachiever. From crushes to bad test grades, she always had a plan, action items, next steps—anything to keep moving forward. Amethyst's quiet resilience was something Rose had always admired about her. Except for right now. Right now it was kind of annoying.

"If I knew what to do, I would've already done it," Rose responded. "Principal Ivy didn't even say what she wanted me to do. She just told me they'd 'consider my progress in Elementary Magic.' What does that even mean?" Rose sat up.

Amethyst bit the cap of her pen as she thought. "Well, she must be talking about the Equinox Test. It's really the only big assessment we have this year. Everyone who passes goes on to Middle Magic." She looked into Rose's questioning eyes. "Right?"

"I thought so, but who knows?" Rose sighed, inwardly shuddering at the memory of the Rogers Middle pamphlet sitting like a wordless threat on the principal's desk.

"Okay, well, this is what we *do* know." Amethyst wrote down *Equinox Test*. "If you do well on the test, Principal Ivy won't have any questions about your progress."

"But next dilemma: The Equinox Test is hard." Rose flopped onto her stomach and looked into Amethyst's eyes. "Or maybe it's only hard for unqualified Magic Bearers like me who deserve to get shipped off to regular-people school."

"I don't think negative self-talk is particularly helpful," Amethyst said, sounding like her mom.

"I don't think that notebook is particularly helpful," Rose snarked.

"Well, I don't think your attitude is particularly helpful." Amethyst gave Rose a close-lipped smile. It was rare, but sometimes Amethyst did flare back at Rose, especially when she was just trying to help and got sass for it.

"I'm frustrated," Rose said in a dejected voice.

"I can tell." Amethyst jotted down *Preparation for the Equinox Test?* and looked thoughtfully around the room.

The Elementary Magic curriculum packed all the core classes into the first four years, and the fifth year was entirely dedicated to the Equinox Test, which was designed to use everything they'd learned up to this point. It was held every year at the end of fall, and none of the students knew what to expect because the assignment was different every year.

After the test, if you passed, winter was spent recharging. Spells were perfected, and technique was sharpened. Once spring came, it would be time for new growth and concepts in preparation for Middle Magic.

Rose wasn't sure what happened if a person failed—she made a mental note to ask her cousin Heather, who was older and would definitely know. Heather always knew stuff nobody else did. Rose could already picture the bleak winter that awaited her if she didn't pass. But more information could give her a bleaker and more detailed idea of what to dread.

"My dad told me that back in his day, he had to make tulips tap-dance," Rose offered, hoping this counted as preparation. "And my mom had to cycle a seed to a bloom in under a minute. Her peonies only barely made it, but if I have to do that I'll probably just end up with weeds."

Amethyst shrugged. "How well we do will impact our placement for Middle Magic classes," she said. "The Check-in will, too." The Check-in was a conversation students had with their Head Teacher where they talked about breakthroughs and problems as they prepared for the test.

"Why can't they just tell us what our task will be and show us how to do it? Isn't it unfair that they just expect us to know what to do?" Rose complained.

"They've spent years preparing us for this test, so technically they have shown us. Probably several times," Amethyst said, tucking her hair behind her ear. "Mr. Lunard says that this kind of independence is what we'll need, not only for Middle Magic, but for the rest of our lives as productive members of the Magic Bearer Community."

Rose very vaguely remembered their Potions teacher saying something like that, but she hadn't been paying attention. Mr. Lunard hadn't been talking to her anyway. Advice like that was for Amethyst and Hugo, the top students in their year.

"Hold on a minute," Rose said as she jolted upright. "I've got an idea. Dawn!" A smile began to crawl across her face.

"Dawn?" Amethyst's brow furrowed.

"Dawn." Rose bobbed her head, seeming to decide something.

"Dawn?" Amethyst still didn't get it.

"Stop saying Dawn," Rose said as she got off the bed and sat across from Amethyst on the floor.

"You started it!" Amethyst huffed. "And I'm not getting up that early until classes officially start."

"Not that dawn. Your cousin Dawn," Rose said as she bit back a smile. "I see understanding is starting to *dawn* on you." Rose laughed. Amethyst didn't.

If Rose had a cousin like Dawn, she would take advantage of it way more than Amethyst did. Just like Amethyst and Rose, Dawn and Rose's cousin Heather were total opposites. Heather was great—if Rose ever needed advice on how to skip school or overthrow the teacher's lounge, Heather would be able to offer a wealth of information on that.

Not Dawn, though. She was a model student but still really cool. She'd graduated last year and was about to start Magic Bearer university. But as the most recent valedictorian, Dawn was on the Committee, a council of leaders in the community who decided, among other things, what the Equinox Test would be, not only for Elementary Magic, but Middle and Specialty as well. Naturally, the Committee was sworn to secrecy until after all tests were completed. Blabbing about it could hurt a person's professional reputation.

"What do you want with Dawn?" Amethyst asked warily.

Rose ignored the rush of excitement and touch of guilt that battled inside her over what to say next. She knew Amethyst wouldn't like her plan. But Amethyst wasn't the one with the Difficult Problem.

Chapter 9
AMETHYST

Amethyst couldn't believe her ears. "You want to what?"

"I want to cheat." Rose never could sugarcoat things, even when Amethyst desperately wanted her to. "Dawn knows what the test is going to be. She'll totally help us out if we ask her."

"Dawn's not Heather, Rose. She won't help you cheat." Rose rolled her eyes, but Amethyst continued. "And anyway, I would never let you even put her in that position. Cheating is forbidden. Besides, they have spells to weed that kind of stuff out, you know." Amethyst folded her arms, a hot flush of anger flaring inside her chest.

"Okay, fine, fine, whatever you say." Rose sounded casual, but her eyes were still in scheming mode.

Amethyst was suspicious. Rose never dropped things this quickly. Either she hadn't been serious to begin with or she was just biding her time until Amethyst came around, which usually involved Rose wearing her down like a piece of chalk scraped against hot asphalt.

Maybe with proper preparation, all this could be avoided. If Rose felt confident going into their fifth year, there would be no need to follow through on any of this cheating business. *A plan*, Amethyst thought. *A plan fixes everything.*

"Come on." Amethyst rolled up her sleeves and pushed back her glasses, heading to the shelf next to her bed to take out a thin rectangular box. Inside were color-coded, neatly labeled bundles of herbs and teas. "Let's go over some simple potions, just to brush up."

Amethyst knew Potions was Rose's weakest subject. Whatever the Equinox had in store, fortifying weak points seemed like a safe bet.

"Oh, great, starting lessons before school even begins—my favorite," Rose mumbled. But she joined Amethyst on the floor, dragging out a large glass bowl from under Amethyst's bed.

Amethyst was already grinding hawthorn, ashwagandha, and valerian root with a mortar and pestle.

"How do you know what to use?" Rose asked in disbelief.

"We learned this our first year." Amethyst grinned at Rose. She was sure if her friend just gave herself a chance, she'd be shocked by how naturally potion making could come to her.

Amethyst poured a pitcher of water into the bowl. The liquid boiled before even hitting the glass, soft steam caressing her cheeks. It was always easy for Amethyst to cast water spells—of all the elements, that one called to her most. Simple spells and charms didn't need words—just focus. But using an incantation was like going from gently tugging something to grabbing it with both hands. Amethyst didn't even need an incantation to work with water. She could whisper with her mind, and the water would listen. It was a rare skill—one she didn't take for granted.

She let Rose sit in her thoughts while she got lost in the familiar motion of sprinkling the herbs, layering them for maximum potency, and gently stirring the brew with a wooden spoon. She even added a dash of honey for taste.

To finish, Amethyst placed a spare book from her desk on top of the bowl, trapping the steam and aroma within. *A few more minutes to let it settle and that should do the trick*, Amethyst thought, biting her lip to keep from smiling. She loved the feeling of a job well done.

"Well, I'm glad one of us is happy." Rose was in full self-pity mode now.

"Oh wow, I hadn't realized there was more than one of us in the room since no one helped me with the potion." Amethyst grabbed two mugs from her desk, one with a smiling wedge of cheese on the front for Rose, and another with a pumpkin doing a handstand for herself. They'd bought them together at last year's Harvest Festival. Rose had insisted they keep them in Amethyst's dorm "for emergencies." So far, emergencies had consisted of a few hot chocolates and the blueberries they'd snuck from the gardens at the end of last term.

"I took out the bowl. Without me there is no potion." Rose was giving herself far too much credit, but Amethyst let her have it. She was having a hard day after all.

Amethyst poured the contents of the bowl into each of their mugs, careful to catch the wilted dregs before they slipped into the cups.

"What's this going to do to me?" Rose looked skeptically at the sweet smoky infusion. It was fluorescent pink, and though Amethyst hadn't used the spice, it smelled vaguely of cinnamon.

"It should calm you down a little, help you relax. Then we can practice again tomorrow," Amethyst said cheerfully.

Rose took a tentative sip and seemed to unwind against her will, her shoulders relaxing and her jaw unclenching.

Amethyst took a sip of her own and smiled. Drinking the potion felt like stepping into a warm bath. Maybe they could figure this out, she decided. If they both put their heads to it, they'd come up with a way to get Rose to Middle Magic.

Chapter 10
ROSE

When Rose got home she tried to duplicate Amethyst's potion not once, not twice, but three times. *Three.* She couldn't even get the water to boil, and eventually gave up and put the kettle on the stove. Even so, though she thought she'd mixed the herbs right, the potion hadn't turned pink, or given that sweet smoky smell. The brew had just curdled together in a lumpy mound.

Rose's mom found her sobbing over the sink, valerian root scattered over the kitchen table.

"I don't even like tea," Rose wailed through her tears, her mom rubbing her back with a confused expression. Rose went to bed not long after.

The days that followed weren't any better. Every day Rose woke up feeling even more desperate than she had the day before.

The quiet smile and sense of accomplishment that radiated from Amethyst as she sipped her potion replayed over and over in Rose's mind. Even if by some miracle she did get to Middle Magic, is this what it would be like? Watching Amethyst soar from achievement to achievement while she just tried to keep up? This was why she didn't do school stuff before the semester started. It just made her feel bad.

For two whole weeks she'd gone to Amethyst's room and stirred potions she didn't really want to make and recited spells she didn't believe she was good enough to cast. And now that she had tried and failed, it was time they visited her earlier suggestion. Their last year of Elementary Magic began in less than twenty-four hours and Rose was getting desperate.

The Difficult Problem ends TODAY.

Dawn is the best chance I have, Rose chanted to herself as she brushed her hair that morning and ate pancakes with her family. Her brother, Reed, glanced at her suspiciously, but she avoided eye contact. Reed wouldn't understand; he'd been too smart for Middle Magic and had skipped it altogether. But not Rose. Rose was fighting for her life just to get to Middle Magic. *Dawn can fix this*, Rose reminded herself. *She'll tell me what's on the test.*

By the time Rose was walking down the hallway toward the school's Central Courtyard, she'd convinced herself Dawn was the *only* way she'd pass the Equinox Test and make it to Middle Magic.

When she knocked on Amethyst's door, it wasn't to get Amethyst on her side but to explain to her that it was either cheat with Dawn or go to Rogers Middle. There was nothing in between. So she was doing this. As her best friend, Amethyst would understand.

"I've thought about it a lot," Rose began without a hello as she barreled into the room. "Dawn is so nice, and she's always offered to help us with our homework. You know she has. That's all this would be. A little hint to put us on the right track. One that will save my entire future."

Amethyst blinked. "I told you, they have ways of telling when people cheat—"

"That's just what they say. They don't actually have any way of finding that out." Rose was almost certain of this. Magic Bearers were servants of Nature, not the bosses of it. They were nothing like those stories about witches and wizards at the Clinton Hill Library. Rose didn't think magic could be used to get information someone wasn't willing to give—and Rose wasn't about to tattle on herself.

"It's the principle of it." Amethyst was shocked, and Rose realized her friend's voice almost sounded disappointed. In her. Like she was judging Rose for wanting—no, *needing*—to cheat. For Rose the stakes were too high to not do everything she could to pass. Amethyst should understand that.

"Dawn won't help you cheat, Rose. You're not thinking clearly!" Amethyst pleaded. "And would you even want to go on to Middle Magic if you weren't ready? That could be dangerous, for yourself and other people—"

"So you don't think I can pass?" Rose's stomach dropped to her shoes. This whole time, she'd thought it was her and Amethyst *together* against the Difficult Problem. Had she been wrong? "That's it, isn't it? You never thought I could do it. You think magic for beginners is all I'm capable of, don't you?"

"That's not what I said. Just consider the consequences. If you're not ready—"

"Not ready?" That little smile of Amethyst's flashed in Rose's mind—the one Amethyst always wore when she'd made a flawless potion or cast a difficult spell—and her insides began to heat. "You act like you're so much better than me—"

"Now, you know that's not true!" Amethyst's cheeks flushed.

"Do I?" Sometimes Rose thought Amethyst forgot that magic didn't come easy for everyone. Rose didn't like the hot prickle behind her eyes. "You act like such a know-it-all sometimes, as if you're so perfect," Rose shot.

"I'm not perfect," Amethyst said as she choked back tears. "But at least I don't have to cheat my way to Middle Magic."

Rose's fury was past boiling; it was molten hot. "At least my mom didn't send me away to be someone else's problem."

A deafening silence fell around the room. Rose's lips clamped shut. She'd just said the unsayable thing. Part of her wanted to swallow back the words and convince Amethyst that she hadn't meant them. But, if Rose was honest, another part of her wasn't ready for apologies. Not when her future was on the line.

Amethyst wasn't the kind of person who broke apart in front of an audience. But Rose saw something inside Amethyst shatter like a bat swinging at glass. The shards stabbed right into Rose's heart. Never in her life had Rose said anything like that, not even on her worst day. Even if she'd sometimes thought horrible things, she never let them out. Not when it came to Amethyst.

"You"—Amethyst's chin wobbled—"are no longer my friend."

"Good," Rose called as Amethyst turned and left her own room. "I don't want to be your friend either."

Chapter 11
LAV

"What do you mean you have to go to schools?" Mrs. Barros untied her apron as she spoke, hanging it on a nearby hook. "Tomorrow is the first day, no? Can't it wait?"

Her shift had ended early, a complication Lav hadn't planned for.

"*School*," Lav sighed, the frustration bubbling inside him. "I have to go to *school*, not schools. And no, it can't wait."

Lav didn't mean for the bite in his voice to sound as harsh as it did, but he'd been at the door with his shoes on when she came home. He'd been so close.

It wasn't his mom's fault that she'd come home early the one time he'd needed to slip out undetected. But still. How many afternoons had he sat here, the drone of TV and traffic his only company? Why was today the day she wanted to be curious about his whereabouts?

He had things to do and a person to see. A person he didn't know how to reschedule with—if he even could reschedule. He'd already done so much prep work, making sure he knew exactly where to go and what to ask. What if he didn't show and everything fell apart? He'd lose his chance to finally be just another student instead of the confused kid always a step behind. He couldn't let this chance be ruined.

"I'm going to school," he announced as he reached for the doorknob, his heart racing from all the possibilities of this going wrong. "I'll be back soon."

"What's so important?" Now it was his mom who had a bite in her voice. "What're you going to the *school* for?" She exaggerated the sound, her eyebrows raised.

"It's a, um . . ." Lav tried to come up with something reasonable. "Study group. A pre-start-of-school study group."

His mom gave him a tired look. Lav knew it wasn't fair to lie to his parents—his mom had no way of knowing if a pre-start-of-school study group was a real thing or not. She hadn't believed school lunches were a real thing when they'd first arrived in Brooklyn. Back home the whole island shut down for a few hours for a midday break. Lav's parents relied on him to communicate these things honestly, which he usually did.

But today, Lav had his reasons for lying. "It's important. Everyone goes. If I don't, I'll be behind."

"Why didn't you have a pre-start-of-school study group

last year?" His mom made her way to the kitchen, pouring herself a glass of water. "Or the year before?"

"Because this is my last year of Elementary Magic." There was urgency in Lav's voice. "And this year matters more than all the others."

That part was true. Too true. Lav had a lot to prove after last year's disastrous end-of-term project. Just thinking about it made his shoulders rise defensively.

They'd had a week to make a potion that caused the drinker to feel joy.

Lav had spent three days just braising carrots. He coated them in thyme and tarragon, boiling bone broth and adding herbs with precision. On the day the projects were due, he'd presented his potion proudly. The aroma had brought a smile to his face, and he'd been sure he'd knocked it out of the park.

Until he'd seen the shocked faces of his classmates. Chamomile Mills had barely held back a laugh, and Amethyst Vern had just looked thoroughly confused, her head tilted to the side as if trying to get a better angle on his humiliation.

It was then that Lav looked at everyone else's cauldrons. They were full of thin, airy herbal mixes and infusions.

They'd made tea and he'd made stew.

On Île Violette, potions could be anything as long as the herbs were right. But here in Brooklyn, that wasn't the case. Only tea was a potion here.

Mr. Lunard, his Potions teacher, had allowed Lav to turn in his stew for the assignment, since technically, he'd never said they couldn't make soup-based brews. But Lav didn't want to be someone who relied on technicalities.

Mr. Lunard had given Lav a passing grade, but barely. Even though his teacher had let out a whoop of delight when he'd tried the stew and asked for the recipe, he'd still warned

Lav to stick to standard potions in the future, which stung.

Afterward, some of his classmates looked at Lav funny. As though he might have fooled the teacher, but he hadn't fooled them. They didn't think he belonged at the school. That because he wasn't a superstar student like Hugo or Amethyst, he must be taking a spot from some other more deserving kid.

Hawthorn Mulberry and Basil Green had even accused him of getting special treatment, a free pass that no one else got. Maybe that had been the moment Lav made up his mind. That was the day he'd decided he was going back home.

Lav's mom slowly nodded her head as she walked over to the microwave timer, punching in numbers as she spoke. "You have thirty minutes to get whatever study group materials are being given out." Her tone made it clear this was not up for discussion. "Once you get home, we'll go over them together."

Reluctantly, Lav nodded—this would have to do. He wasn't sure where he was going to get fake worksheets for the fake study group, but that wasn't a priority right now. He just had to get to school for his appointment. He'd figure out the rest later.

Cold sweat beaded down Lav's spine as he calmly waved

goodbye to his mom and shut the door behind him. Then he sprinted through the hallway, down three flights of stairs, and onto the pavement, each step a countdown to the plan that would get him back to Île Violette for good.

Chapter 12
ROSE

Today is the actual worst day of my life, Rose thought as she fled through the courtyard.

The hurt look on Amethyst's face haunted her as she walked aimlessly toward an exit. They weren't friends? That didn't even sound possible. Rose and Amethyst were like a bagel with schmear. There couldn't be one without the other. What was Rose now, just cream cheese? Or worse—a plain bagel?

Why in the world had Rose said she didn't want to be Amethyst's friend? In the moment, Rose had definitely had her reasons. But now, in *this* moment, she couldn't remember what they were.

Rose felt oddly exposed as she roamed through the empty hallways, the late-afternoon sun persistent as it shone through the glass ceiling. She couldn't understand how everything had gone so wrong. Her plan had been so straightforward—tell Amethyst that getting a hint about the test from Dawn was her only option, figure out a way to contact her cousin, and finally skip happily into the sunset straight to Middle Magic. Together. The togetherness was a very crucial part.

Things had spun out of control so fast. And what if Amethyst was right and Dawn wouldn't help Rose after all?

Heather would've definitely given Rose the answers if she'd had them—not that anyone would trust Heather with information like that. But Dawn was more like Amethyst. If she wouldn't help Rose, then all the words Rose had thrown at her former best friend were for nothing. And she couldn't take them back.

Lost in thought, Rose tripped over a step and nearly went face-first into the river. She missed it by inches, colliding with the smooth marble floor instead. The sound of koi fish giggling made her cheeks run hot. As she ungracefully got back on her feet, Rose finally looked around at her surroundings.

The usual glass ceiling had vanished and been replaced by shiny green leaves the size of Rose's head and vines as thick as her arm. Golden sunlight washed over the canopy and the gem-colored birds that perched on branches and flitted through the leaves. The September air outside was warm but didn't match the thick heat of this corridor.

I have to tell Amethyst I found a jungle, was Rose's first thought as she bit her lip in excitement. But, glumly, she realized that ex-friends didn't tell each other about cool discoveries. They didn't do anything together.

The leaves suddenly seemed less shiny, and all Rose wanted was to go home—her journal was going to be shocked by all the things Amethyst said to her. Absolutely shocked.

By the classroom names—Advanced Portal Physics, Soil Biochemistry, and other stuff she could barely pronounce— Rose could tell she was in the Specialty Magic wing. She didn't know her way around this side of the school. As her eyes scanned for an exit, they caught on a sign at the end of the hall that read CORRESPONDENCE ROOM. A thought tugged at her brain.

If she could get ahold of Dawn and get the answers she needed, maybe she could rescue this day from being the worst one ever. She could calm down and properly make up with Amethyst. She would even accept the apology she was sure that Amethyst would give her once she realized Rose had been right all along and Dawn really was the answer to all their troubles. *This is genius*, Rose thought, smiling to herself. She could already picture Amethyst's reaction when she told her Specialty Magic had its own rainforest.

Triple-checking that no one was around, she slinked toward the Correspondence Room. Rose was positive Reed had told her about the Correspondence Room before, not that she'd listened very closely. He'd needed tools from it for a research project. He was an actual genius and *loved* to talk about his research, telling Rose tons of very specific information she was never going to use.

Information I thought *I was never going to use.* Rose sighed, sweating in the stuffy humidity that seemed to press in on her.

If Reed knew what I was doing, he'd be so disappointed, Rose thought, then immediately pushed it to the back of her mind. Reed trusted Rose. Even if it was pretty boring, Reed telling her about magic way above her skill level was technically forbidden. If anyone found out, her brother could get in a lot of trouble.

He'd even told her about Heart Leading. Rose had struggled to keep up as he described how everyone she loved was connected to her just like she was connected to them, and the steps she'd need to Heart Lead.

"Like how fungi connect the entire forest floor. It's the same thing for us," he'd explained, face lit with excitement. "You can't lose something you're always connected to. Lead with your heart, then find me or Mom and Dad if you need us. This is important stuff to know, just in case of an emergency."

Rose had nodded along as if she actually cared. It meant a lot to her that Reed trusted her with that knowledge—even if she'd never be skilled enough to actually Heart Lead. If she could do that, she probably wouldn't be dealing with the Difficult Problem.

As she approached the door to the Correspondence Room, Rose shook out her shoulders. What would Reed think of her plan? Would he understand? And why did she feel like such a criminal? She wasn't hurting anybody.

If she was lucky, she'd find a Communication Portal. They looked like shoebox-sized wooden frames wrapped thick with ivy. But she wasn't going to get her hopes up— Communication Portals were uncommon because of how difficult they were to spell.

Rose remembered reading about them in a textbook once. They seemed amazing. All you had to do was hold the portal, think of someone, and they would appear in the frame as if they were on a screen, with or without a Communication Portal on the receiver's end. She'd asked her dad if she could get one for late-night chats with Amethyst in New Jersey.

"Absolutely not," he'd declared. "It's a very rude practice to force communication on someone who has no way of declining you."

But at the moment it seemed like a great way to get in touch with a certain cousin of a certain friend, well, former friend, who could really help Rose out right now. At least then this day wouldn't be a total loss.

When this plan works out, everything will be fine again, Rose told herself as she twisted the doorknob.

Chapter 13
LAV

Lav thought he heard the door creak open and the faint patter of footsteps.

You're being paranoid, he reminded himself. In the five minutes he'd been in the Correspondence Room, he'd also thought he'd heard the swish of a tail and a soft thud—as if some small creature were lurking in the shadows monitoring him. He'd ignored that, too.

Today was not the day to be scared. Today was *the* day, plan day—and he only had fifteen minutes left before he had to get home. He brushed aside all other noises and focused on the choppy voice coming through the other end of the Communication Portal. A voice Lav hadn't heard since the weeks he'd spent in Chicago over the summer. He was finally talking to the only person he'd met in America who had understood his desire to take control of his future.

Who else would've been willing to give him the equal footing he needed? Who else would've told him how to pass the Equinox Test?

"What's that about singing?" Panic began to rise in Lav's stomach as the connection was broken by more static. He'd risked too much for this to go badly. "I need to know that to pass. And you're sure that's what the assignment's going to be, right? Hello? Can you hear me?"

Lav's whisper carried through the empty Correspondence Room, the soft glow of the device the only brightness in the space. He'd left the lights off as he'd entered, not wanting to alert anyone to his presence. Lav tapped the Communication Portal against his hand, hoping to fix the fuzzy audio.

He hadn't realized these things could get bad reception. Did this happen to everyone or just to him? His classmates had probably played with Communication Portals as toddlers and knew all the tricks. Maybe there was a button he needed to press? His fingers, slicked with sweat, felt around for any clues.

As he looked up in irritation, he froze. Staring at him, equally shocked, was Rose Vera.

Lav didn't know Rose that well. She was in his year, had curly hair, and usually hung around with Amethyst. And she was loud. Too loud in Lav's opinion. Her voice carried.

But right now she was as silent as a shadow. She'd clearly just walked into the room, and Lav wasn't sure how much she'd heard. He dropped the Communication Portal on the shelf, silencing it. Regret immediately washed over him. Not only had he made himself look guilty of something, but he'd also lost the connection, which he wasn't sure he could get back. He hoped that at least, with the lights so dim, Rose wouldn't recognize him.

"Lav? Is that you?" she asked in a shaky voice. Lav sighed. Clearing his voice, he finally spoke. "Hi, Rose."

The silence stretched between them uncomfortably. It wasn't exactly against the rules to be in the Correspondence Room after lab hours, even if Elementary Magic students were only supposed to come to the Specialty Magic wing under teacher supervision. To Lav's knowledge, it wasn't even against the rules to use a Communication Portal. But using it alone, in the dark, before school had even started . . .

It didn't look good. He'd just wanted to have this conversation in private without anyone snickering and laughing at his questions—he got enough of that in class.

Lav didn't think anyone even used this room. Didn't they all have Communication Portals at home? Wait a second, what was *she* doing here? Lav raised a brow. If it was suspicious that he was in the Correspondence Room, then it was also suspicious that Rose was here, too.

As the seconds ticked by, Lav felt around for the fourth-year worksheets he'd found by the school river and hastily shoved in his back pocket. He hoped he could pass them off as acceptable "study group materials."

But first, he fumbled for an explanation to give Rose. Should he just admit his family didn't have a Communication Portal at home? That he had no one to ask for advice about school stuff other than a near stranger in Chicago who he'd only met a few times?

What he'd done wasn't cheating, Lav had been assured of that—he was just thoroughly preparing for the Equinox Test. In Chicago, Lav had been told students used Communication Portals to reach out to tutors and other students for help all the time. Plus, his teachers had always encouraged the students to take advantage of the knowledge within their community. That's all he'd tried to do, even though he hadn't actually heard anything helpful before being interrupted.

Lav thought he was more than owed a head start. Everyone else got one, whether they admitted it or not. This was his chance to go above and beyond, to focus his full energy on actually executing a project, not just trying to understand all the unsaid rules that his classmates automatically understood. With his success this year, his parents would finally see that he'd gotten everything he could from school in the States and was ready to go home to Île Violette.

Whatever happened, he wouldn't let himself forget that he'd deserved this chance.

Rose cleared her voice, pulling him away from his thoughts.

"Hi, Lav . . . I didn't mean to interrupt you." She licked her lips nervously. "But I should get going. I'm already late for dinner." Not waiting for a response, she turned and ran out of the room.

Lav exhaled. *Did that just happen?* He wasn't exactly upset about not having to explain himself. Hopefully Rose wouldn't say anything. He took two deep breaths before he left, closing the door gently behind him. He glanced left and right—the hallway was completely empty. Rose was nowhere to be seen.

Lav thought about the bits and pieces he'd heard through the Communication Portal. *Sing? What could that possibly mean?* The word danced in his head, bringing up unwanted images of him forced onto a stage with a microphone in hand, his knees shaking with terror.

Just the thought of it made his throat go dry. He must've heard wrong. There was no way the Equinox Test had anything to do with singing. This was supposed to be a school for magic after all.

Lav sighed, sure a sleepless night haunted by off-key notes and high-pitched screeches awaited him—after he finished filling out his fake pre-start-of-school study materials, of course. Shoulders sagging, he didn't waste another second as he turned on his heel and sprinted for the exit.

Chapter 14
AMETHYST

The next morning, Amethyst found herself staring at the small lake in the corner of the South Arboretum. It was tucked away from the area's main feature, a sprawling stone theater where the school held ceremonies like today's Welcome Assembly. The glass ceiling above encased the grounds like a second sky and reflected the clouds onto the lake's surface. Surrounding the water were hundreds of gem-colored tulips and thick willow trees, pixies bustling from their dangling branches like twinkling insects.

As Amethyst searched for her seat, she noticed Mr. Kneely and a few mer-students chatting softly from within the lake's tranquil depths. A small part of her wanted to dive in and join them.

She continued along a stone pathway that was cluttered with classmates and teachers. Amethyst overheard a few murmuring about a skirmish with the Under City that had been all over the morning news. She'd have to ask her mom about it the next time they had lunch together. Right now, all she could focus on was the nervous excitement that bubbled inside her.

Amethyst always looked forward to the first-day-of-school Welcome Assembly. It was pretty much the same every year—Principal Ivy gave a welcome speech, and then Mr. Sol, their History teacher, would talk about the legacy of Magic Bearers in Brooklyn and how proud they should be as students of this craft.

It reminded Amethyst of why learning to carry magic was so important to her. It wasn't something new being planted in the world, it was something that already existed being watered. Like a dormant seed brimming with life in the right conditions. While sprouting was easy, growing was hard. It took a lifetime to learn how to master.

Amethyst liked to compare it to learning to read sheet music. Once a person could identify different notes, they started to hear them everywhere: in the whine of a taxi horn, the clatter of a fork, even in the click of a pen. The noises weren't new, but noticing them was. For Amethyst, magic was the act of calling on those notes to turn them into songs. That's what Elementary Magic had been at least.

And here, at the Brooklyn School of Magic, students expanded and honed that awareness. It made Amethyst feel like she was part of something so much bigger than herself—just one of many voices singing a song they were writing as they went.

Amethyst finally found a smooth stone with her name carved into it and sat, wiggling with excitement. This assembly marked the beginning of the new school year. Soon there would be new books to read and puzzles to solve—Amethyst truly couldn't wait. She smiled at nearby students, recognizing most of them. They were seated alphabetically by year so she usually sat with the same groups of people.

Amethyst froze mid-wiggle.

She'd completely forgotten. She looked at the vacant seat to her left, heart sinking. ROSE VERA was carved into the gray stone, just like AMETHYST VERN had been carved into hers. Of course she would be sitting next to Rose. They'd always sat next to each other, but even if the order hadn't changed, their friendship status had.

Amethyst hadn't spoken to Rose since their fight. This was the first time they hadn't spent the morning of the first day of school together. Usually, Mr. Vera would make them waffles and hot chocolate, hers with extra whipped cream and Rose's with cinnamon sprinkled on top. It was their guarantee for a perfect first day.

But so far, the quietness of life without Rose had been startling, like the silence after someone abruptly stopped laughing. Her morning had felt long and lonely. Amethyst had done her best to fill the time tidying up her room, getting her younger sisters situated, watching the news, and feeling jittery enough about it to make an unplanned trek to the library. Luckily, Felix, the school cat, had been there to help soothe her nerves.

He'd been tucked on the bottom shelf between spell books on the second floor. Felix was cream-colored and fluffy, like a cotton swab, but was considerably shyer than Jax, the purple neighborhood cat who was constantly slinking around. Jax was very popular with students.

As they waited for the assembly, Felix wound through the rows of students, stopping to let Amethyst rub his chin. *At least I have you, Felix,* she thought. Still raw from her fight with Rose, Amethyst remembered how special she'd felt to be someone like Rose Vera's best friend. Rose could light up an entire room like a bonfire. Hers was a presence a person felt instantly.

"Hey, Amethyst." Chamomile Mills smiled from the row ahead, turning in her seat to talk. "How was your summer?"

It took Amethyst a minute to respond. How *had* her summer been? She'd been too distracted by the fight to figure out how she'd answer these kinds of questions. "It was great. I, um . . . I went down the shore with my sisters a lot. We mostly hung out on the boardwalk." *At my mother's insistence,* she didn't add.

"'Down the shore'? Wow, you really are a Jersey girl now. You even talk like one! Ha!" Chamomile Mills laughed, Amethyst did not. "Where's Redhead Rose anyway?"

Amethyst couldn't believe anyone still used that old nickname.

Back in their first year, Rose couldn't figure out how to turn her hair orange in Charms class. They weren't even really changing it, just the way light reflected around it so it seemed orange without actually *being* orange. Amethyst had done it without much thought, as had the rest of the class. But Rose couldn't manage it, even with Amethyst covertly trying to help her.

"I can't do this," Rose had huffed with a scowl. She wasn't embarrassed even a little bit, just frustrated. It was something Amethyst respected. If she'd been publicly unable to complete an assignment, she would've melted with shame.

"Everything all right, Rose?" Mr. Kneely had asked as he swam over, his once long brown locs now the color of a pumpkin.

The entire class was looking at Rose now. They had looked at Amethyst, too, since she was sitting right next to Rose. Rose had lit up under the attention, while Amethyst shrank back.

"Everything's fine. How are you?" Rose had asked as if they were chatting in a café.

Mr. Kneely had offered Rose a small smile. "How's the assignment coming along?"

"It's going great," Rose had responded with zero hesitation. Mr. Kneely had looked questioningly at Rose's chocolate-brown curly hair. Without missing a beat, Rose had added, "My hair is actually orange. I've been doing a charm all along to make it look brown."

A few of their classmates had snickered. But Amethyst could tell they weren't laughing *at* Rose, they were laughing

with her. The ability to get a crowd on her side was Rose's ultimate superpower.

"Is that so?" Mr. Kneely had crossed his arms, clearly not believing her.

"Yes, it is. I'm a natural redhead as a matter of fact. You can ask anyone," Rose had said, nudging Amethyst in the ribs.

"Oh, ugh, yeah, um, I guess." Amethyst hadn't convinced anyone.

Mr. Kneely had asked to see Rose after class and moved on with his lesson, but apparently some of their classmates still called her "Redhead Rose." Usually they said it with admiration.

Chamomile looked around the arboretum. "Don't you and Rose normally come to these things together?"

Amethyst shrugged, offering a closemouthed smile. Someone called Chamomile's name and she turned back around, saving Amethyst from having to explain.

Great, Amethyst thought, *now everyone will know I'm friendless and alone.*

"Almost friendless," she amended as Felix purred at her feet. She absentmindedly patted the cat's head as more and more students filled the theater and she waited for the assembly to start.

Amethyst began to tap her toes in anticipation. The empty spot next to her was starting to feel like a challenge. When the seat was filled, what would she say? What would she do? She couldn't just let "Redhead Rose" walk all over her and call that a friendship.

Amethyst appreciated Rose's blaze, but she knew she had her own light, too—it just shone softer, like a gentle sunrise over a calm sea. She'd never expected someone like Rose to even want to be her friend. They'd grown up together but had only started becoming close during their second year of school, right as Amethyst was ripped away to New Jersey. Those first few weeks, before they'd decided to try boarding, she'd spent two hours on a bus commuting to and from the city.

Amethyst hadn't been able to do after-school hangouts or weekend slumber parties anymore. She'd held back tears when she heard the other girls talking about their adventures together over lunch or during study time. She'd been sure that her friendships would wilt away because of the distance, and some of them did.

But Rose hadn't forgotten about her. She'd gone out of her way to include Amethyst and had even come to New Jersey a few times to visit. Even though it took a little extra work, Rose thought Amethyst was worth it. Knowing their friendship meant as much to Rose as it did to Amethyst had lit a quiet confidence in her. It made Amethyst walk with her head a little higher and her back a little straighter.

Except now Rose wasn't a part of her life anymore. Trying to keep from squirming, she sat on her hands and blew out a loud breath. Felix pranced onward, weaving through the crowd.

As she looked around the crowd of students gathering to begin a brand-new school year, all the air drained out of her. The arboretum seemed to shrink and close in on Amethyst. Was she even still breathing? The last, straggling students were filing in. And Amethyst, a defiant set to her mouth, turned her head pointedly in the opposite direction as Rose Vera took her seat.

Chapter 15
ROSE

Rose wanted to look at Amethyst. She wanted to grab Amethyst's hand and say, "I'm so sorry. I messed up. I didn't mean any of it, especially the part about your mom. Please, I'll do anything—forgive me." But Rose didn't. Instead, she stared straight ahead and acted like the person she knew best in the world wasn't sitting right next to her.

"Good morning, students." As Principal Ivy began speaking into the mic, Rose was too busy not looking at Amethyst to notice what she was saying. They sat through the same welcome speech every year. Rose didn't think she was missing much.

It was Principal Ivy's deep sigh that made Rose finally look at the stage. Worry colored the educator's expression, and without even realizing it, Rose scooted closer to Amethyst. Something was wrong.

Principal Ivy continued, a forced smile on her face. "Today I find myself especially grateful to start this new year with you all. Know that despite any external conflicts, the Brooklyn School of Magic will always be a safe haven for its students." She looked up from the papers in her hand. "You will always have a place here."

Rose turned her head to the corner of the arboretum, where the principal's gaze seemed to hover. Rose couldn't see anything but flowers and that little lake. She began to turn toward Amethyst to ask if she saw anything out of the ordinary, but Principal Ivy cleared her throat.

"This was not the beginning-of-year speech I had planned on giving. Yet circumstances demand that I address the problems we as a community face, both outside these walls . . . and within them." She seemed sterner now, looking each student in the eye. "Yesterday in the late afternoon, the Correspondence Room was opened and a Communication Portal was used."

Rose was sure she'd just turned to stone. She'd never sat so still in her life.

"The portal was used to gain restricted information on the Equinox Test." Principal Ivy scanned the crowd, lingering on Felix the cat for a long moment before continuing.

Rose thawed as she followed the principal's gaze farther down the front row to a familiar student in the third-to-last seat. Her eyes burned into Lav's wavy brown hair. *Had he been cheating?*

She could feel Amethyst's icy glare on her, but Rose was too fixated on Lav to give it attention.

Back in the Correspondence Room, Lav's eyebrows had pointed at her accusingly, and she'd started to panic. *He knows everything,* she'd thought. *What I'm going to do, who I'm going to call, that I'm going to cheat, that I'm a terrible friend, everything.* Under the interrogation of Lav's eyebrows, Rose had begun to sweat. It was a miracle she'd even been able to escape.

But she *had* escaped, Rose remembered with a breath. And she'd never even called Dawn on one of the portals. No, the

only person who'd used a Communication Portal that day had been Lav. And he'd done it alone in the dark and had quickly dropped it once he'd realized she was standing there.

Rose hadn't heard who he'd been talking to. Through the static, there'd been a faint echo of a voice that had sounded a little bit familiar, but then silence once he'd dropped the frame. Silence Lav had been in no hurry to fill, as if getting caught had startled the words right out of him. As if he'd had something to hide. As if *he* was the one who'd been cheating.

A shocked laugh escaped Rose's lips. *That sneaky little fraud,* Rose thought smugly, even though she'd also planned to cheat. But unlike Lav, she hadn't actually done it. Rose was too proud of her detective skills to notice the absolute fury pouring from Amethyst.

As far as Rose was concerned, she didn't have anything to worry about. Lav was the guilty one, not her.

Chapter 16
LAV

The heat started at the tips of Lav's ears and then crawled to the rest of his face.

Why does he look like that?

"If anyone has any information on this incident, we ask that you please come forward. As Magic Bearers, we have a duty to one another and our community to make honest and fair choices," Principal Ivy continued. "Beyond teaching you how to hone and use magic, a core part of your education is learning how to make responsible decisions and use good judgment.

"Neither was done in this situation. To the student or students involved, please come forward so this matter can be dealt with."

Did she just look at me? She looked at me. I didn't do it—well, I did, but it wasn't cheating. I was told repeatedly it wasn't considered cheating. Lav's breathing was becoming shallow as his mind whipped into a frenzy. Who was he kidding? Who would believe that he genuinely hadn't known it was cheating? Absolutely no one.

He'd thought everyone else knew what the Equinox Test would be—their parents and older siblings had taken it, after all. But not Lav. He'd just been catching up, trying to get a sense of what to expect. Now, knowing what he'd done *was* cheating, Lav felt confused and betrayed. How had he believed some stranger in Chicago so readily? Was he that naive?

I believed it because it was everything I wanted to hear, Lav realized. He was annoyed. It wasn't that he couldn't keep up. Everyone else just had a head start. Using the portal and getting some answers was a simple and easy way for Lav to finally come out on top. To prove he'd learned everything he could here and was ready to go home. How had he convinced himself that any of it was a good idea? He disintegrated in his seat under Principal Ivy's stern gaze.

"Are you okay?" Magnolia Bartlett whispered from the seat next to him.

"Yes." *No, not at all.* "It's allergies." Lav had never had allergies a day in his life.

He struggled to control his breathing and listened.

"Now that we've discussed this, I'd like to turn the mic over to Mr. Sol to continue with our Welcome Assembly."

Already whispers had spread through the crowd like mist on the ocean.

"Hello, students," Mr. Sol began. "As most of you know, the Brooklyn School of Magic began as a small windowsill garden."

"Someone cheated?" Hugo murmured, his eyes round as if he'd just witnessed something tragic.

Mr. Sol cleared his throat loudly. "And from that windowsill our knowledge grew, and our magic along with it."

"Who was it, do you know?" Jasmine leaned forward from the next row to continue the conversation.

"I bet they'll get expelled!" Chamomile looked almost happy about it.

Expulsion was not the way to get back to Île Violette. Lav knew that for a fact. If he got expelled, his parents would probably stick him in Rogers Middle—a fate he *refused* to accept.

There's no way Principal Ivy knows it was me. Lav slid his sweaty palms under his thighs, the heat creeping from his face to his entire body. *Nobody does. Except . . .* The heat suddenly turned to ice.

Someone did know. It was at that exact moment he felt eyes on the back of his head like lasers singeing his hair. He peeked over his shoulder. Rose Vera was staring pointedly at him—and she was smiling.

Chapter 17
AMETHYST

A few rows behind Lav, Amethyst's thoughts were racing a mile a minute. She hadn't believed Rose would really go through with it. Putting Dawn in that position, risking her reputation, her future—after how hard she'd worked? It made Amethyst sick.

And had Dawn actually helped Rose cheat? It was like Amethyst didn't know anyone's true character anymore. Like she'd never known them at all. She let out a small laugh, though nothing was funny. Absolutely nothing.

Amethyst had to talk to her cousin. But to say what? *Hi, Dawn, I thought you were a better person than it turns out you are. My mistake.* It's not like Dawn owed it to her to be some kind of role model. Dawn was off at college; the trivial drama of one test for Elementary Magic probably meant nothing to her.

Amethyst squinted at Rose and pushed her glasses farther up her nose, as if that would make everything clearer. Despite her smug little smile, Rose seemed antsy and on edge—exactly how someone who'd been caught cheating *would* act. It was all the confirmation Amethyst needed.

She wished she could be the kind of person who didn't care, who could let people hurt her feelings or disappoint her and forgive them instantly. Rose was like that, always eager to let things go.

But for Amethyst, each slight was a betrayal she couldn't let herself forget. Because when it happened again—and it *always* did—she'd have no one to blame but herself. How many times had her mom canceled lunch or weekend plans, with Amethyst forgiving her only to be let down again and again? And how many small comments from Rose had Amethyst brushed away only to have her heart ripped out in the end?

Amethyst's heart began to race. First her mom, then Rose, now Dawn. Was Amethyst doomed to lose everyone in her life, one way or another?

Something lodged in her throat, and Amethyst knew she had only seconds until the tears came. She didn't even hear Mr. Sol's words as she walked as casually—and as quickly— as she could out of the arboretum and into the nearest bathroom. Her sobs erupted just as the door swung shut.

Chapter 18
LAV

The assembly dragged on as if Lav wasn't preparing to have the most important conversation of his life. Rose didn't know it yet, but how she handled this would either doom or save him. Once the droning of teachers finally ended, everyone flooded the halls and he set out on his quest.

As soon as he spotted Rose, she disappeared, snaking through the trees and hopping from stone to stone across the stream that ran the length of the hallway. Lav followed, his eyes glued to the curly hair ahead of him. Rose seemed to be on a mission of her own, but that would have to wait.

Lav needed her to understand that he hadn't meant to cheat. *What can I say to get her to understand that?* Lav thought hopelessly as he raced to catch up to her.

"Hey, Rose! Can we talk?" Lav panted, fear and nerves jingling inside him like a set of keys.

Rose skidded to a halt and scowled at him. She was about to let him have it when the bathroom door next to them opened and Amethyst stepped out, hands wiping her red eyes.

Rose stared at Amethyst, Amethyst stared at her feet, and Lav looked between the two, confused.

"Are you all right?" Rose asked, her voice small. She reached her arms out to hug Amethyst but then dropped them abruptly and looped her fingers around the straps of her backpack.

"I didn't think you'd really do it," Amethyst said, speaking more to the floor than anyone in particular. "But I guess I really shouldn't be surprised." She looked up then, her brown eyes focusing on Rose.

"I'm sorry," Rose began with a whine. "I shouldn't have said—"

"Not that." Amethyst wouldn't even look at her.

"Then, what are you talking about?" Rose asked, genuinely confused.

Lav wished they could relocate this talk somewhere other than the middle of the hallway. A few students were staring as they made their way to morning classes. Chamomile Mills pointed at the wisteria-covered clock that hung on the wall and raised her eyebrows. The bell was going to ring any minute.

"You cheated!" Amethyst hissed.

"No, I did not." Rose's response was instant. "It wasn't me. It was—" Just as she was about to point her finger, she saw

Lav's fervent headshake from the corner of her eye. "Someone else," Rose finished unconvincingly. "Thinking about doing something and actually doing it are not the same thing."

"Yeah, right. Rose Vera took the easy way out. Is that really such a shock?" Amethyst bit out unkindly.

Lav found that uncharacteristic of her. He didn't know Amethyst well, but she didn't normally talk like that. Regardless, he needed to tell Rose his side of things and get to class.

"Can I just talk to you for a second?" Both girls turned toward Lav as he spoke, his cheeks flushing. "Rose, I mean. Can I talk to you, Rose?"

"Why yes, you can," she responded, staring pointedly at Amethyst. "Assuming you're not going to accuse me of anything . . . unlike *some* people." Rose stalked down the hallway, not waiting to see if Lav followed.

The morning bell rang and a shuffle of students swarmed into Mr. Sol's classroom, but Rose headed instead for a small sitting garden dotted with rocks, Lav close on her heels.

"Wait up!" he called as she marched into the garden and slumped onto a bench.

"I'm not a bad person!" Her voice echoed through the vacant halls. "And I'm not a cheater."

Lav was surprised not to hear accusation in her voice. Rose sounded more hurt than anything. Maybe she didn't know—

"You're the one who cheated."

"Not on purpose." Lav's voice was pleading, and even though the halls were empty, he still looked over his shoulder and kept his voice low. "I didn't realize—"

"Lav Barros? Rose Vera?" The scent of salt air and cinnamon wafted toward them as Mr. Kneely peered up from a bend in the river that snaked through the garden. "Shouldn't you two be in class?" A piping hot cup of coffee rested in Mr. Kneely's scaled fingers, his waist-length locs floating on the water's surface and his merman's tail just out of view.

I Be-Leaf in you!

"Um . . ." Rose stared unhelpfully at Lav, who soundlessly moved his mouth for a second before clearing his throat.

"Yes, I just needed help with, um . . . homework. Yesterday's homework." Lav shook his head. *He* didn't even believe what he was saying.

"Yesterday's homework, on the first day of school?" Mr. Kneely squinted at them, his green sweater crisp and dry despite being half-submerged. "I think not. There's too much on my plate with Under City matters to escort you myself, but I trust you're both heading straight to your lessons before my generous mood changes."

Rose and Lav shared one desperate look before rushing to their classroom. Lav caught Mr. Kneely's soft sigh as he descended underwater.

"I'll explain everything, I promise," Lav whispered from the corner of his mouth as they slunk into Ms. Rainwater's classroom. His dad needed him to pick up some books from Mr. Vera anyway. That would be the perfect time to explain.

Lav wasn't sure who Rose was beneath her loud voice and big personality, but he hoped she was the kind of person who would believe him.

Chapter 19
AMETHYST

Amethyst's eyes narrowed as Lav and Rose snuck into class. Ms. Rainwater, their Head Teacher, paused briefly before she continued.

"As I was saying, this year's assignment . . ."

Amethyst could see their teacher's lips moving, her expressive eyes dancing and hands flowing along as she explained what the Equinox Test would consist of. But Amethyst heard nothing except a dull roaring in her ears.

She glanced sideways at Rose and thought of a thousand mean, terrible things to say, yet felt guilty for every one of them . . . and then mad at herself for feeling guilty. She looked back to Ms. Rainwater, shaking her head. Amethyst needed to pay attention to important things like school and not useless things like friendship and betrayal and abandonment. If she wanted the Blossom Award, she would have to do better. She *would* do better.

"Are there any questions?" Ms. Rainwater asked as she looked around the classroom.

Amethyst cringed. Had she just missed the most important instructions of her life for the biggest assignment of the year?

Her hand shot up of its own volition, her instincts saving her since her feelings were clearly set on sabotage.

"Ms. Rainwater, I would like clarification on the assignment," Amethyst said evenly.

"Of course." Her teacher gave her a kind smile. "For this year's Equinox Test, you must each demonstrate how to make a flower sing. It's intentionally broad to allow room for creativity and exploration. Your flowers may be potted or rooted, and greenery may accompany it if you wish, but the song itself must come from the flowers. You'll have the entire fall to prepare, presenting your projects at the end of the semester."

Amethyst's eyes lit up, her brain screaming with ideas. It was a natural progression, the logical part of her reasoned. For all of Elementary Magic they had been listening to Nature, and now it was time for Nature to listen to them. But how? Already spell combinations, soil recipes, and seed arrangements flitted through her mind.

Lessons were Amethyst's happy place, where things made sense and had concrete due dates and expectations. There were no surprises, nothing that couldn't be rationalized. The total opposite of people, with their unpredictable choices and intense feelings.

Amethyst welcomed the distraction. Because with a fresh sheet of notebook paper and sharpened pencil, she could take over the world.

Chapter 20
ROSE

Rose could feel Amethyst burrowing into schoolwork. It was what she knew best. But that left Rose alone in their feud. And a one-person feud was the loneliest place to be, Rose decided as she slumped in her chair.

She tried to pay attention. Ms. Rainwater seemed nice enough. Rose vaguely remembered her specialty being tropical vegetation. The seven-foot-tall monstera and the unreasonable warmth of the classroom seemed to say as much.

So much jumbled in Rose's head. Did Ms. Rainwater know that the test was Rose's last chance? Did she realize that how Rose performed in this classroom, on the Equinox Test and whatever else was thrown at them, would decide whether she ascended to the ranks of Middle Magic or plummeted to the depths of Rogers Middle?

She needed to focus. Rose refused to let anything distract her. Not Lav's cheating. Not Amethyst's hurt feelings. Not the suffocating heat of the room or the way it made her upper lip sweat. Nothing. The stakes were too high, and Rose was all out of chances.

Someone, probably Hugo, raised their hand from the opposite side of the classroom.

"Is this the same assignment whoever cheated already got the answers to?" *Definitely Hugo.* Rose rolled her eyes. "Isn't that an unfair advantage?" Hugo insisted. He didn't notice the way Lav lowered down into his nearby seat, but Rose did.

Ms. Rainwater nodded. "I understand where you're coming from, but Principal Ivy reviewed all the information we know about the incident thoroughly and felt there was no need to alter the assignment."

"But—" Hugo shot out of his seat, physically moved by the injustice of it all.

"This Equinox Test is planned months in advance. Lots of research and resources go into every aspect of it." Ms. Rainwater's voice was stern but gentle. "It's not something that is altered lightly—not when the outcome of the assignment impacts the progression of your education."

Rose could've sworn Ms. Rainwater was staring at her, eyes bright with accusation. Rose blinked, and when she looked again, Ms. Rainwater was nodding as Hugo prattled on—as if she hadn't moved a muscle.

"I hear your concerns, but I can assure you the test is and remains fair." Ms. Rainwater's tone made it clear this was the end of the discussion. Hugo plopped into his seat and crossed his arms.

Rose rolled her eyes again. He didn't even have anything to worry about. Hugo was top of the class, right up there with Amethyst. He would pass with flying colors like he always did. Rose hadn't thought smart people could be insecure, but that's sure what it seemed like. She didn't understand why they felt the need to doubt themselves so much. Other people had real reasons to feel incapable, people like her.

I should be the one worried about every possible disadvantage, Rose thought, the realization seeming to press in on her.

She glanced at Amethyst, who was already furiously scribbling in that new notebook of hers, glancing up periodically as Ms. Rainwater began a lesson on orchids. *I should be scribbling furiously in* my *notebook*. Only, Rose wasn't even sure she'd brought a notebook—it was the first day of school, for goodness' sake! Every year, she was surprised her teachers dove into lessons right away.

Amethyst paused in her writing and peered at Rose as

if she could feel her panic rising like an overflowing glass. Rose's heart leapt. Despite all they'd said, some part of Amethyst still cared about Rose, even if at the moment it was buried deep down inside her. Amethyst began to lean over, but caught herself and pressed her lips together as she turned back to the board.

For now—and maybe forever—Rose was in this alone.

**

After classes on Friday, Rose lay face down in bed. She couldn't believe how badly her first week of school had gone. She'd tried to get started on figuring out the Equinox Test assignment, not that it was much of a choice. Rose didn't have anything else to do. She and Amethyst still weren't speaking, so her social life was nonexistent.

Rose had even stayed up late one night and read through *Sapling Symphony: A Guide*. Unfortunately, it wasn't until she had tried and failed three different melody spells that she realized the book was mainly about trees. And for the assignment, trees didn't count as flowers—she'd asked.

The book really should've been called *Rose Vera, You're Wasting Your Time Because* Sapling Symphony: A Guide *Is Not about Flowers Singing*. All she'd done was accidentally sprout a fluorescent yellow branch from the Japanese maple

outside her window. Its presence seemed to taunt her. She couldn't even figure out how to get rid of it.

On Monday, Rose decided that she couldn't admit defeat so easily. Before school she lined up a row of dandelions from her backyard on the kitchen table. She'd used tweezers to keep their root systems intact as she'd moved them into a mug. Once in their new home, Rose pushed them to a sunny spot, then pulled out Reed's harmonica.

People had been speaking to dandelions for centuries, probably longer, telling the flowers their wishes as they blew fuzzy petals into the breeze. After listening to people for that long, dandelions had to know how to talk by now. And singing was just talking with a beat. Rose had never played her brother's harmonica before but had wanted an excuse to try for a while, and this was the perfect moment to give it a go.

She took a deep breath, and then blew into the small metal instrument with all her might. The sound that came out reminded her of someone banging on piano keys all at once. Rose stuck with it, trying with mild success to play the "Happy Birthday" song. The dandelions didn't give her any feedback, but Rose was having a great time.

Or at least she had been until the kitchen door slammed open.

"IS THAT MY HARMONICA?" Reed yelled. "Who said you could borrow it?"

Rose grabbed the mug and ran into the backyard, harmonica in hand. But the dandelions flew to the ground behind her and were immediately clobbered by her brother's feet as he chased after her.

That Wednesday, Rose's attempt at being studious didn't quite work out either. She'd tried to pay attention in History class. But with the warm sun resting on her face through the window, Rose had wanted nothing more than to leap out the door and run to the nearest sun-drenched meadow for a well-deserved nap. She hadn't been sleeping well lately.

Rose was smart, she knew that. But her flavor of smart was active and responsive. Rose learned by doing, not hearing about what others had done. She'd held on for as long as she could before her mind started to wander. Mr. Sol was theatrically pointing at a globe while his voice seemed to drift farther and farther away.

". . . the pixie revolution of the seventeenth century shook the Netherlands and, really, the entire world. Unassuming tulip bulbs grown in the Ottoman Empire were imported to Holland and turned out to be so much more important than anyone could have known. This is when it really gets good." He lifted his foot onto his chair and his eyes bulged, glued to unseen tulips from hundreds of years ago.

Rose scanned the class, taking in the engaged faces and furious scribblings of her classmates. Vines crawled slowly across the floor onto Mr. Sol's desk, some department memo getting delivered, no doubt. She sighed. What was wrong with these people? Who cared about a pixie revolution from a million years ago. Weren't current events, like the tension with the Under City, more important? Rose didn't really know much about any of that beyond what she overheard at school, but if anything were to boil over, that would actually affect them—unlike pixies and tulips. Rose distantly wondered if the Under City had anything to do with her canceled beach trip. She'd nearly forgotten about that.

Yawning, Rose glanced at the sign posted above Mr. Sol's door: MAGIC IS A SEED UNTIL IT'S GIVEN WHAT IT NEEDS. *This isn't what I need,* Rose decided as her eyes glazed over and slowly shut.

The day couldn't end fast enough after that.

All Rose wanted was her couch and a mug of piping hot chocolate. But as she was leaving, she spotted her koi fish friend, Kyle, in the campus river and stopped to chat with him. She didn't understand much about the Freshwater and Saltwater drama he vented about, but she nodded along sympathetically all the same.

Rose was completely depleted when she finally opened the front door of her familiar brownstone. She was greeted by the sound of her dad's voice filtering in from the kitchen. He didn't usually come home from the restaurant this early.

Rose slipped off her shoes in the foyer, sighing with relief at the proximity of her couch, when something snagged her attention. A pair of crisp white sneakers, far too neat to be Reed's and too small to be either of her parents'. They rested unassumingly next to one of her dad's old duffel bags.

Rose's hearing seemed to sharpen then, and when she heard

a second voice reply to her dad, she hurried to the kitchen. She knew that voice. That voice had chased her down in the hallway on the first day of school and then aggressively avoided her. But what on earth was that voice doing in her home?

Chapter 21
ROSE

Rose's thoughts and feet halted as she came face-to-face with Lav Barros.

He was chatting casually with her dad, as if they did this all the time. Lav sat straight-backed in a wooden chair nestled in the breakfast nook while her dad waved a spatula emphatically as he spoke.

"I spent some time there after university," her dad was saying. When it caught the light, his short, curly hair was so black it looked purple, except at the temples, where sky-blue wisps had begun to sprout. "Île Violette is one of the most beautiful places I've ever seen," he continued, turning as he realized Rose was there and giving her a smile in greeting.

"And you still chose to live in the city?" Lav responded. A half smile hung on his face but turned into a tight-lipped shrug as his eyes slid to Rose and then back to her dad.

"Of course, of course." Mr. Vera's attention was now on the crackling skillet as he poured thick batter in heaping dollops into it. "Brooklyn is my home. It's where I feel closest to Nature."

"Really?" Lav's eyebrows shot up in surprise. "All these buildings and people—I've never felt farther from Nature." He looked down as he said it, and Rose could tell this was a connection he was sad he'd lost.

"Buildings and people are Nature." Mr. Vera gave Lav a grin as he flipped the batter on the stove. "Without Nature's generosity, none of it could exist. Too often we forget that. Here, and even in the Under City, we're all benefiting from Nature—even if we don't always agree on how to use that generosity." He grabbed a platter from the cabinet. "Without Nature there would be no taxis, no skyscrapers, none of it." As he filled the platter, a smile grew on his lips. "DeKalb Avenue is my Grand Canyon," Mr. Vera said, placing a steaming plate of pancakes on the table.

The golden buttery goodness took all of Rose's attention. Breakfast for dinner was her *favorite*. But Lav was nodding his head, hardly noticing the treasure that lay before him.

"I guess I never thought of it like that," Lav was saying as Rose grabbed a plate, slathered extra butter on her stack, and reached for the warm maple syrup her dad had placed on the table.

I feel closest to Nature on a full stomach, Rose thought as she took a fluffy bite.

Then she turned to the unexpected guest. "Why are you here?" she asked with her mouth still full.

Her father frowned at her from the stool he'd perched on, the mug of tea hovering just below his lips. "My friend Lav stopped by and I invited him to stay for dinner," he said, as if it was the most normal thing in the world.

"Your *friend*?" Rose stared at Lav, who was tentatively eating a pancake; he didn't seem sure how to go about it. "Why are you acting like you've never had a pancake?" she asked, distracted by his unusual behavior.

Lav's cheeks colored subtly, his tan skin flushing as he put down his knife and fork. "Because I haven't," he said, barely loud enough for Rose to hear.

"YOU'VE NEVER HAD PANCAKES?" She hadn't meant to shout it or for it to come out like an accusation. But Rose couldn't picture a reality that didn't include pancakes fresh from the skillet.

"Just because it's normal for you doesn't mean it's normal for everyone else," Lav shot back, a defensive bite in his voice.

"You're probably more used to crêpes," Mr. Vera said.

Lav's eyes lit in recognition. "Yes, exactly." A slow smile

bloomed across his face. "My grandmother makes the best in the world." He gestured toward the pancakes. "These taste just like them, only thicker and fluffier."

"High praise," Mr. Vera said, giving him a slight bow.

Just then, Rose's mom came down the stairs. She had onyx hair that flowed to her waist, a defined jaw, and broad shoulders. She'd been a dancer once, and still moved with catlike grace.

"Smells delicious!" she said, giving Rose's dad a peck on the cheek and sliding her arm around her daughter for a half hug. Then her eyes lit brightly in Lav's direction. "And we have a guest!"

"Oh, you mean you don't know Dad's *friend*?" Rose said flatly.

Mr. Vera ignored her. "This is Lav, Aster's son."

They sat around the table chatting about food from around the world, all the different kinds of desserts that were essentially cake, and, briefly, about school. Rose and Lav made eye contact before Rose rushed the conversation in a different direction.

"Are we ever going to reschedule that beach trip to Coney Island?" Rose pulled at the first thing she could think of to switch topics. "It's going to get too cold soon."

Her parents glanced at each other, her mom frowning. "Maybe next season. We have so much going on with the Harvest Festival coming up. A lot still needs to be collected from the garden. The squash and tomatoes really thrived this year," she noted.

Later, when their plates were empty and the table cleared, Rose meandered into the sitting room. She was finally within sight of her beloved couch and savored the feeling as she plopped onto it. She could hear Lav thanking her father emphatically for hosting him. If she rolled her eyes one more time, Rose was sure they'd fall out.

When she felt a slight movement of the cushion beneath her, Rose didn't have to turn to know Lav had joined her on the couch.

Rose's parents were still in the kitchen chatting over a pot of tea. Out of earshot. She could finally begin her interrogation. "What're you doing here? And how do you know my father?" she asked matter-of-factly.

Lav shrugged. "One of my dad's jobs is working in the garden at Butter Crust, and sometimes I help out." That was the restaurant that Rose's family owned, located just a few blocks from their home. "He's been super into algae lately, and your father has a collection of really hard-to-get volumes he's lending to my dad. So since I needed to talk to you anyway . . ."

Rose's dad had an extensive library in the attic. He and Uncle Jared, who happened to be dean of the Chicago Academy of Magical Arts, regularly traded volumes and tracked down editions together on topics ranging from desert sandstorms to the history of peaches. She didn't ask why Lav hadn't just said from the beginning that he was running an errand for his dad. His feelings on the matter were very clear: his shoulders hunched, his eyes fixed firmly on the ground while he chewed on his lip.

Rose would have to mark today in her diary—the day she'd actually kept her mouth shut. It was a rare and monumental occasion. She'd have to get herself a little treat.

A laugh came from the kitchen, and Lav looked up. "It's cool that your parents are home like this," he said.

"My mom handles business at Butter Crust during the day, and as head chef, my dad preps in the morning, then works in the kitchen with the rest of the cooks at night." She glanced at the clock—he'd be heading back out any minute. "I guess it's nice that they're here when I get home from school."

"My dad works nights, too." Lav looked around the sitting room, seeming to take it all in. "And mornings. So does my mom."

"Then, when do you see them?"

"Not often," Lav said matter-of-factly.

They were quiet for a long moment. Then Rose prompted, "So you needed to talk to me . . ." She'd just wanted to know why he was in her kitchen—she hadn't needed his whole life story.

"Yeah. About . . . everything . . ." Lav began. "I wasn't . . . I didn't realize . . ." Lav's lips kept moving but no sound escaped. Eventually he took a deep breath and looked Rose in the eye. "I was told everyone already knew what was on the Equinox Test. Everyone but me. And I thought everyone had Communication Portals at home that they used all the time. That it was fine to ask parents, older siblings, neighbors—anybody who knew anything—for help. Our teachers are always saying, 'Our community is our biggest resource.' Why is the test any different? It's not like my parents know how things work, even after a few years' living here. And she said—" Lav furrowed his brow in frustration.

She who? Rose wondered, but didn't ask. She could tell he was exhausted by all this.

"I need you not to tell anybody that I was the one using the portal. Not yet." Lav sighed. "I promise I'll come clean about everything, just not right now. I really thought I was just catching up . . ."

What Rose thought was that Lav's eyes looked tired. Too tired. "All right," she said, surprising herself. "I won't say anything." Rose didn't think he deserved to get in trouble and was about to tell him so, but Lav stood, glancing at the clock.

"Thanks," he muttered as he headed toward the door, slipped his shoes on, and grabbed the duffel bag. "I should get going. I want to give my dad these books before he heads to his evening shift."

Rose parted with her precious couch to stumble after him. "Well, get home safe," she said, then cringed at herself.

She'd heard her mom say that a million times but realized it sounded weird coming from her.

"Thanks," Lav said with bunched brows and a small laugh.

"I take it back," Rose said as Lav walked through the door, turning on her front stoop. "Get home however you get home, and I'll see you when I see you." There, that sounded much more her.

It seemed Lav thought so, too, because he smiled to himself as he walked away. Rose watched him round the corner before she shut the door.

Now Rose knew for sure: Lav had definitely tried to cheat. She wasn't sure if he'd found out anything helpful, though. It certainly hadn't seemed like it. But either way, she wasn't going to tell on him. And Rose couldn't muster any guilt about it.

Amethyst would feel duty bound to tell Principal Ivy, but Rose didn't. Anyway, she decided she liked having this secret. Lav's secret. A small bundle of information tucked aside just for her. The curve it gave her lips felt warm. A secret with a secret smile to go with it.

Chapter 22
LAV

The sun hung patiently in the sky as Lav began his trek home. It wouldn't set for a few more hours. He thought of Rose's beach trip request and wondered how long the warm weather would stick around. The start of autumn was not so far away. *And the Harvest Festival along with it*, Lav thought.

For him, the Harvest Festival was still as intimidating and overwhelming as it had been that first year he'd moved to Brooklyn. Everyone in the community came with a bounty to offer: kale as long as an arm or apples as big as pumpkins. For someone like Rose, it was probably the highlight of the year. She'd show up with baskets full of produce from the restaurant garden and an entire army of people carrying food and handing out plates. Lav could almost taste Butter Crust's flaky biscuits and steaming squash soup.

The festival was different for him. His family would show up empty-handed, like they always did. Their cramped apartment was either totally dark or boiling with sunlight.

They didn't have a backyard or space to breathe, let alone plant. Nothing could grow in a place like that.

Lav knew he wasn't the only one who would show up with nothing to give. The entire point of the Harvest Festival was for the community to support one another. Nature was generous and, as Magic Bearers, they had an obligation to pay that generosity forward. But it was an ugly feeling to receive with nothing to give. Watching his parents gather an array of the vegetables and fruits offered with nothing to trade but warm smiles made his cheeks heat and shoulders tense.

He tried to shake off those thoughts as he climbed the stairs to his building.

"Lavender, is that you?" his dad called from the kitchen table as Lav unlocked the door.

"I got your books," Lav replied, placing the duffel bag on a chair.

Mr. Barros patted his son's back and rifled through the bag. "Thank you, thank you! There's even more here than I'd hoped." His dad was giddy as he unfolded his reading glasses and gently took out each volume to examine.

"I stayed for dinner at the Veras'." Lav settled into a chair beside his dad, his elbows resting on the table.

"Oh yeah?" His dad looked up from the title he was squinting at. "What'd you eat?"

"Pancakes." His dad's brows knit together in confusion. "They're like thick crêpes. Very tasty."

"Nice. It's good to try new things," his dad responded lightly, before going back to the books.

Lav stood and got a glass of water, then sat back down and got out his homework. He tapped his pencil, the sound harsh and loud in the quiet room. He stood again.

"What's going on?" His dad leaned back, taking off his glasses.

"Nothing." Lav dropped into his seat and kept his eyes glued to the paper in front of him. The Harvest Festival was still haunting him, as much as he didn't want to admit it. This was the kind of thing he'd talk to his grandmother about. But they weren't scheduled to meet for another few days. Lav had been kind of avoiding his parents lately. He hadn't been sure how to tell them about the cheating incident, so he'd decided to just not tell them anything at all.

"You've been so quiet lately. Is something going on? Something at school?" His dad glanced down at the homework sheet in front of Lav.

"NO!" Lav said a little too forcefully. His dad raised his

eyebrows. "No, it's not school. It's the Harvest Festival."

"Oh? What about it?" Mr. Barros crossed his ankles.

"Doesn't it bother you?"

"What?"

"That we have nothing to contribute?" Lav wasn't sure what he expected his dad to say.

His father leaned forward, pushing aside his books so he could be eye to eye with Lav. "We keep this community running as much as anyone else," he said sternly, but not unkindly. "Someone has to till the soil before others can use it in their gardens. Someone has to gather and dry seeds before they can be planted and monitor the seedlings for disease and pests to make sure the entire crop isn't lost." Lav knew the work his parents did was crucial, knew the calluses on his dad's hands were well earned. But still.

"But why does that someone have to be us?" Lav asked.

His dad stood and gathered up his books. "That's for your mother and me to worry about. It's our turn to work hard now so that one day, it'll be your turn to harvest." He squeezed Lav's shoulder and went to get dressed for work.

Their first year in New York, the guilt for everything his parents endured on his behalf—for his future harvest—had only just begun to take root inside Lav. Now, three years later, it felt like an entire guilt-forest had grown. Guilt-grass, with a guilt-stream, and guilt-birds flitting from guilt-tree to guilt-tree.

Lav turned back toward his homework. He was so tired of feeling guilty. But he wasn't sure how to stop.

Chapter 23
AMETHYST

Amethyst had not slept well. In fact, she'd slept quite terribly. But she couldn't afford any more bad days, not after the bad week she'd already had.

During one of her History lessons, Amethyst had been so busy conducting an imaginary conversation with Dawn in her head that she'd frozen when Mr. Sol called on her.

"Amethyst, why have pixies preferred bulbs over seeds since the Middle Ages?" he'd asked, eyes alight. He clearly thought he was giving her an easy question.

If Amethyst had been paying attention, it would've been. Instead, she'd been thinking about how she'd confront Dawn about helping Rose cheat, and how Dawn might then turn things back around on Amethyst for not tattling on Rose to the principal. It had been a very heated fake conversation.

"I, um . . ." Amethyst trailed off, her eyes bouncing around the room for some kind of clue. To her left they landed on Rose, who was clearly asleep. Here Amethyst was disrupting her own education because of Rose's decision to cheat, and Rose had the nerve to be carefree and unbothered enough to take a nap. Amethyst's lip began to shake, and angry, hot tears gathered in the corners of her eyes.

"Bulbs became more available in the Middle Ages because of trade, and pixies came to prefer them as they're more spacious than seeds and there's more room for their nests," Lav cut in. He shot Amethyst a quick look. Lav must've thought he was saving her, but if he'd just given her more time, Amethyst could've answered on her own—she didn't need his help. She didn't need *anyone*.

Mr. Sol nodded approvingly and continued his lecture on tulips, but Amethyst was too furious to listen. *We aren't even supposed to be learning new material during our fifth year. What*

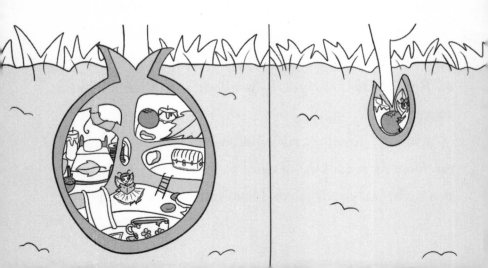

does the history of tulips have to do with making flowers sing?
Amethyst wondered, unwilling to see the lesson as a possible clue for the assignment.

Since classes weren't going as planned, Amethyst refocused on the Equinox Test, spending the next few days planting and replanting pots of flowers. A new home with the right magical properties might encourage them to break out in song. She'd drowned a marigold in a confidence potion she'd whipped up, thinking if the flower believed in itself, that could encourage it to sing. Nothing happened, not even when Amethyst tripled the recipe.

Then she'd switched tactics with a bunch of hydrangeas, casting a spell to make them sway as if their stems were dancing. Amethyst had even played her favorite salsa music, getting curious looks from other students in the courtyard as she worked. It was a long shot, but sometimes when Amethyst heard a song she liked, she'd dance without even thinking, and sing along, too. Maybe the same could be true for flowers.

But the hydrangeas didn't so much as hum. Absolutely nothing happened, other than Magnolia Bartlett whipping her head around as she shook her arms to the beat.

Losing her patience, Amethyst thought about charming

herself to look like a flower. Then she could just sing on her own when she presented her project. But deep down, she knew that wouldn't count. *She* wasn't a cheater. And also . . . she didn't know how to do it.

Nothing was going the way Amethyst wanted it to. If she kept this up, forget the Blossom Award, she might not make it to Middle Magic at all.

"That can't happen!" Amethyst burst out so heatedly the next morning that her hairbrush clattered to the floor. She picked it up, embarrassed even though she was alone in her room. This was a new day full of new opportunities. Opportunities that were ripe and ready to help Amethyst pass the Equinox Test with flying colors and make her mom proud.

Amethyst took one last look in the mirror. Then she grabbed her bag and headed for breakfast, hoping to get in some studying while she feasted on scrambled eggs and toast. Everything was going to be just fine.

In her first class of the day, Charms, Amethyst accidentally turned her pencil case invisible, which made it really hard to take the pop quiz her teacher sprung on everyone. During her next class with Ms. Rainwater, they'd been allowed to ask questions about the Equinox Test, but Amethyst stayed quiet, saying nothing. Though she had many questions, she couldn't remember them. And the detailed notes she'd written down were tucked safely away in the pencil case she couldn't find. So while everyone else was fighting for time to get help with their projects, Amethyst sat frozen at her desk.

"Okay, the bell is going to ring any minute," said Ms. Rainwater as she quieted the class. "Are there any last questions before we finish up for the day?"

As the rest of the students talked and packed up their books, Amethyst began to panic. Time was running out and she hadn't made any progress. If she didn't at least try to get some help now, she was doomed. So, with absolutely no context or elaboration, Amethyst blurted out, "Is it possible hydrangeas don't like salsa music? Do you think they'd like classical better?"

The class fell silent, except for Hugo, who couldn't contain his snickering. Amethyst didn't make outbursts in class. That was a Rose thing, not an Amethyst thing. Luckily, the bell rang—and saved her from the misery of having to explain herself.

She tried to make a stealthy exit, mortified for even attempting to speak. But Ms. Rainwater was too quick.

"Can you explain your question?" she asked Amethyst. "What happened to your hydrangeas?"

"Nothing. It's fine," Amethyst insisted, still walking toward the door. "Everything's fine."

It wasn't until afternoon break that Amethyst truly accepted that everything was not fine. She took refuge in the library, hoping just being close to knowledge would rub off on her. She'd move in here if that was the case.

The library was ten stories high with books wrapped around every wall. Columns of bookshelves stretched from the marble floor to the domed glass ceiling, where the afternoon sun was shining generously. One of Amethyst's favorite things to do was meander around the stacks of books, walking in wide circles and just seeing what caught her eye.

But not today. Today, Amethyst slumped into a chair and pulled the ones she'd already borrowed toward her. *The Secret Lives of Succulents* and *Alone with Aloe Vera* offered nothing helpful.

Amethyst reread the assignment she'd taped to the front of her composition book: "In order to move on to intermediate coursework, commonly referred to as Middle Magic, students are required to produce independent, musical sound from the seed-bearing part of a plant (also known as a flower). Plants may be potted or vase occupying."

The empty notebook it was taped to seemed to mock her lack of progress.

Amethyst looked around the spacious building. Plenty of her classmates were in here, leafing through almanacs and spell books—or at least pretending to—while they chatted. There were silent study areas, but talking was encouraged in the library.

Mrs. Trestle, the librarian, rolled past Amethyst. The towers of books on the cart she pushed swayed ominously.

"Did you find everything all right, dear?" she asked, grabbing an armful more from a nearby shelf.

"Yes, thank you," Amethyst responded with a painted-on smile.

"Good, good," Mrs. Trestle said as she continued rolling her cart. "Bring that Rose Vera next time you stop by. She's a hoot." Amethyst knew the librarian was a big fan of Rose, as most adults were. "Remember, you can't know alone!" With that she rounded the stacks, no longer close enough for Amethyst to tell her just how alone she really was.

Amethyst's empty table seemed to stretch on for miles. She wouldn't let this faze her; she felt like it was almost a challenge. *I can know alone*, Amethyst thought as she sat up, glasses sliding down her nose. *They wouldn't assign an impossible task*, she encouraged herself. But flowers, like all plants, had their own thoughts and desires. They weren't inanimate objects to manipulate—they were alive. A living thing she had to somehow boss around.

The laughter from a nearby table broke her concentration. Amethyst glared at the fourth-year study group. They were doing more talking than reading. Amethyst was grateful *she* didn't have a distraction like that. Nope. No friendship or laughter over here, just laser focus and academic excellence.

Amethyst quietly sighed. Maybe if she shoved the jealousy down far enough, she would forget it was there. All those fourth years had one another; she had no one *and* no progress. Maybe she really couldn't know alone.

But, as Amethyst glanced at the vacant seats around her, she had to try.

Chapter 24
AMETHYST

After a long day of fruitless studying, Amethyst wasn't looking forward to dinner with her mom and sisters. *But if I can just get out of my head a little bit, have a change of scenery, maybe I'll be able to approach the Equinox Test with a fresh perspective,* she convinced herself as she walked toward the restaurant.

They'd chosen one of her favorites, a small Magic Bearer–owned spot tucked away in Clinton Hill. The owner always gave Amethyst a free breadstick. She began munching on it, savoring the garlic deliciousness, as her sisters chattered endlessly. Their lives as second years sounded much more thrilling than her own, and she fell into silence as she poked her spaghetti around half-heartedly.

"And then I told her," Julie continued, "that if Jade said she didn't charm my pinky nail green on purpose, then I believed her. Everyone at snack time wanted to see my hand afterward, but it faded after only a few minutes."

"You handled it really well," Sage added, turning to

their mom to see what she thought. Sage's teddy bear also joined them for dinner. It sat in its own seat with a napkin tied around its neck and a single uncooked noodle in front of it.

"Yes, you did. I'm very proud of you." Ms. Vern reached out and squeezed Julie's hand, and Julie instantly beamed like a small sun. "You showed a lot of wisdom. I know plenty of adults who would've let something like that ruin their entire week."

"Are pinky nails a big issue at the Firm?" Amethyst commented. They were the first words she'd said all night.

"I wish," her mom responded, a dark look momentarily shadowing her features.

"Are things all right?" Amethyst sensed something was off. "At work? Everything quiet in the Under City?"

"Quiet enough, although I hear some things have made it on the news. It's just Under City Council disagreements. It will blow over soon," Ms. Vern said, taking a bite of ravioli. "Sage, I think Mr. Bear might still be hungry after that noodle. Maybe we should get him a nice big slice of chocolate cake?"

Amethyst's sisters squealed, completely oblivious that their mom had totally avoided the question. It bothered her more than she let on. She never understood how her mom expected the world from her daughters but offered very little of herself in return. But maybe only Amethyst felt like that. Maybe she was the only piece of this family that didn't fit, and that's why she had to work so hard to pretend that she did.

Amethyst looked out the nearby window at the city silhouetted against the night sky. She reached for her glass of water, but instead of taking a sip, she just held on to the cool glass slicked with condensation. It felt comforting for some reason. What would it mean if her mom's work *wasn't* going well? Did that mean their time in New Jersey was coming to an end, and boarding at school along with it? The thought didn't fill Amethyst with the joy she thought it would. She was so lost in what-ifs that she missed her mother's words at first.

"I'm so excited," her mom was saying, her fork punctuating every word.

"Yeah, me too," Amethyst said absently. She glanced at her sisters—one of them must have said something to impress their mother, but both Julie and Sage were looking back at her expectantly.

"We'll have to go shopping before the ceremony to get something special for the big day." Her mom was smiling, pride gleaming in her eyes.

She's talking about the Blossom Ceremony, Amethyst realized, breaking out in a cold sweat.

She nodded along but couldn't think of anything to say about it for the rest of dinner and most of the night after that.

Chapter 25
ROSE

As the school year went on, Rose tried to buckle down on her lessons. But in Potions class, when Mr. Lunard was teaching how to make a plant-growth serum, Rose couldn't help offering her opinion.

"This seems like a lot of work for fertilizer," Rose pointed out to Mr. Lunard as he wrote the steps out on the board.

"Miss Vera, this is exactly the kind of information that may be useful for the Equinox Test," he responded evenly.

Rose sighed and tried to follow along as Mr. Lunard demonstrated the bubbling recipe for the class. That had been her first mistake.

First, she prepared the potion's base. But when she dropped the mustard leaves into her cauldron, they just sputtered. Amethyst's cauldron was boiling. So was Hugo's. Even Clover Stanley, a fourth-year student who had skipped ahead in the Potions curriculum, had the contents of his cauldron simmering. Rose's cauldron was completely flat, not even smoking.

She certainly couldn't ask Amethyst for help. And if she asked Hugo, the smug look on his face would make her so angry her ears would close.

"Hey, how'd you do that?" Rose whispered to Clover.

"Huh?" he replied, looking confused.

"The potion. How'd you get yours to boil?" Rose asked with a little more force. Why couldn't he just help her already?

Then, suddenly, as Clover leaned closer to take a look at Rose's potion, the sticky yellow liquid began to boil all on its own. Only it was just one big bubble rising to the surface, growing and growing until it began to fizz. And then it popped . . . right in Clover's face.

He shrieked like a cat. Chaos erupted. Mr. Lunard started screaming, "Settle down! Settle down!" to the class as the fizzing noise got louder. Rose inched away from her now empty cauldron. The contents were stuck to Clover's face like a mask. It was horrifying.

But Mr. Lunard cast a complicated spell that cleaned the serum off Clover's face and even charmed back the eyebrows and eyelashes that had been singed off. Then he gave Rose a hard stare.

"Young lady, I think you'd better go see Principal Ivy," he

ordered before leading Clover out of the classroom and to the nurse.

Rose felt somewhat guilty. But really it was Clover's own fault. He shouldn't have been looking into Rose's cauldron in the first place. She'd just asked him what to do; he should have used his words. Certainly the incident hadn't warranted a trip to the principal's office, which is why Rose hadn't gone. She'd spent the remainder of that period in the hall, catching up with Kyle the koi fish, who seemed more stressed than usual.

Studying at lunchtime hadn't been going any better. Rose had started setting up camp at a table in the cafeteria. Normally, she tackled her assignments in the library with Amethyst, where she got to crack jokes with Mrs. Trestle the entire time. But Amethyst had claimed the library as her territory early on in their feud.

After a month of not speaking to her former best friend, Rose still wasn't used to these quiet meals. Quiet except for Lav, who now sat across from Rose most days and wasn't the chattiest person.

On a pedestal next to their regular table sat a collection of curated plants meant to bring peace and tranquility. There were bonsai and violets and five kinds of lily, but Rose couldn't stop staring at a small potted cactus, its yellow flower sprouting on top of it like a little hat.

For days, she'd been giving this making-plants-sing thing an effort. Maybe what she needed was a plant that was as prickly as she felt. She took a swig of water, cleared her voice, closed her eyes, and then, leaning inches from the cactus's pointy bristles, whispered, "Sing."

Rose leaned her ear down close, in case this was a

soft-spoken cactus. She'd tried this same tactic with a sun-flower, a dandelion, and most obviously, her namesake, rose. If she was "one" with anything, it'd surely be that. Sadly, it turned out the humming she'd heard came from Lav, not the rosebud. She'd scowled at him until he stopped.

Rose stared intently at the cactus, prepared to give it all the time it needed to follow her command, when she heard a shrill sound from across the room. Chamomile Mills was laughing, and she wasn't alone. Sitting across from her, glasses and all, was Amethyst.

Rose had assumed she'd started eating in the library. But here she was, sitting with Chamomile Mills! That cut Rose deep. Amethyst didn't even look in Rose's direction.

As she reached for the cactus she'd been coaxing, she accidentally grabbed a peony planted inside a glass jar. She didn't notice herself taking off the lid, let alone the little sign stuck in the soil that read PLEASE DO NOT TOUCH in big, bold letters.

Before she knew it, she'd ripped off every single petal, shredding them to bits with her eyes locked on Chamomile Mills. It wasn't until she was shaking that Rose looked down and found Lav jostling her arm to get her to stop. Then he pointed at the fine print on the sign: *This flower, presented on behalf of the Fairy Guild, is a symbol of the unbreakable bonds of the Magical Community. May we, like the plants who teach us, continue to grow and flourish.* PLEASE DO NOT TOUCH.

Well, it was a little late for that. If the flower was so important, it should've had better security. "Why is that flower even here? Fairy territory is in the Bronx. Everyone knows that."

"I'm afraid the Fairy Guild will not be amused, no matter their location," a weary voice called from behind Rose. It was Principal Ivy, and she was giving Rose a look that bordered on concern. "I do think, though, that they'll probably issue you a formal Forgiveness. *If* you write an apology. I'd be happy to forward it on your behalf."

Great, extra work I won't even get graded on. Yay. Rose sighed. "Fine, whatever."

"Now, Miss Vera, would you mind coming along to my office?" the principal continued. "We have some important matters to discuss."

Rose froze. She was sure Principal Ivy was about to drag her kicking and screaming to Rogers Middle, despite the gentle smile the administrator was giving her as she led Rose to her office.

"After our initial conversation, I wanted us to have a chance to talk one-on-one," Principal Ivy began. "How are you?"

"Peachy," Rose answered. She was spinachy at best.

Principal Ivy nodded slowly as if deciding which tactic to use. *Will it be a pep talk first, then the rug pull, or will she just go for it?* Rose wondered.

"Have you ever seen a strawberry grow?" Principal Ivy leaned forward on her mahogany desk.

Here we go. Rose took a breath. "No," she responded, crossing her arms. She actually liked strawberries. A lot. Rose picked wild ones on Butter Crust's rooftop garden in the summer, but she'd never seen the plant's journey from seed to fruit.

"I've always thought that strawberries were Nature's love letter."

Rose tried to lock her eyes into her head to keep them from rolling as Principal Ivy smiled and reached for her windowsill. She grabbed a small terra-cotta pot.

"At first, strawberries are tiny buds. Then they start to bloom into the most delicate little flowers." Principal Ivy gestured toward the small yellow-and-white blossoms. They were dainty little things. "And then, like all flowers, they seem to wilt. But that's not what it's actually doing." She gently lifted a flower. "It's growing."

Rose leaned closer, the corners of her elbows bumping against the desk. Nearly hidden by wilted petals, the centers of the little plants had begun to push out and turn into yellow-tinted berries. The ripest among them had red streaks beginning to peek from the stems.

"Given the right conditions, they keep growing until they're perfectly ripe. And once they're ready, I'll put them in my famous wild berry jam." Principal Ivy's eyes glittered. Her jam was a blue-ribbon winner every year at the Harvest Festival. "Wonderful people, like yourself, will eat it and go out into the world and do amazing things. You'll take the best parts of that strawberry with you. And it will keep growing inside you and in everything you go on to do."

Was Rose supposed to want to be a strawberry? She wasn't sure.

Principal Ivy seemed to read the thoughts on Rose's face and sighed. "You have so many blooms ahead of you, even if you don't realize it yet."

Rose wondered if those little flowers knew what was coming or if they were blindsided like she always was. Did they see their neighbors and suspect? Did it hurt?

"Your teachers say you seem a bit distracted in class lately.

Is everything okay?" Principal Ivy tilted her head to the side as she asked the question.

"Yup, totally fine." Rose's tone was casual in a rushed way that ended up not sounding casual at all.

"If you ever want to talk more, about how fine everything is, I'd be happy to listen." Principal Ivy seemed to measure her next words carefully. "We may have approached this situation in the wrong way. The discussion about switching schools was never meant to intimidate you or make you feel as though you aren't good enough." She looked Rose in the eye. "And I'm very sorry if it did."

Rose squirmed in her seat.

"I hope this conversation gives you some reassurance that I and all your teachers want you to succeed." Principal Ivy offered her a close-lipped smile. "And we're going to do

everything in our power to make sure you do." As she spoke, the door to her office gently opened in silent dismissal.

Rose wished she could do that—control things with just a thought. That was *real* magic. If she ever got to Middle Magic, maybe one day she'd be able to. With a sigh, she stood, slinging her bag over her shoulder as she turned to leave.

"Just a minute." Principal Ivy pulled out the top-right drawer of her desk and rummaged around. A second later she pulled out a tiny jar. The label read IVY FAMILY JAM with a smiling strawberry drawn across the front. "Have a great rest of your day," the principal said as she placed the jar in Rose's outstretched hand.

Hours later, as Rose nibbled on her toast, smothered generously with what turned out to be some truly delicious jam, she wondered if maybe Principal Ivy was right. Maybe right now she was wilted and droopy, but one day, maybe . . .

Rose wiped her sticky, crumb-covered hands on her pants and headed up to her room.

Maybe one day she'd shock them all.

Chapter 26
ROSE

Rose and Amethyst continued to ignore each other as the official start of fall inched closer.

One particularly brisk morning, Ms. Rainwater was drawing diagrams of petal structures on the board, and the twitch of Amethyst's pencil on paper was grating Rose's nerves.

It was the day of their Check-ins, and she wasn't ready. No one was ready. Well, except Hugo, whose seedling was humming softly. His conceited little smile was beyond annoying.

Rose wondered if Lav was making any progress. She hadn't seen him at lunch lately, and a few times he'd even missed school altogether. That wasn't uncommon—with the summer season ending, there were harvests to tend to. Ripe produce waited for no one. Lots of kids missed class to help their families and came in early or stayed late on other days to catch up. Lav might even be at Butter Crust helping his dad in the garden, though Rose doubted it. Neither of their parents would've let him miss school. But if he wasn't helping with the harvest, where was he?

"Psst." Rose turned, but the message wasn't for her. Chamomile Mills was handing Amethyst a pencil from the seat behind her.

"Thanks, Cami," Amethyst said, smiling softly and taking the pencil.

Rose fumed.

What happened to Amethyst's pencil case? How'd "Cami" know she needed one? Are they reading each other's minds? We're not supposed to do that until Specialty Magic! I should report her to Principal Ivy. We're friends now. SHE GAVE ME JAM! I wonder how "Cami" would feel about that. She doesn't have jam.

Rose couldn't help herself. "'Cami'? You two have nicknames now?"

"What was that?" Amethyst hissed. These were the first words they'd spoken to each other since The Incident.

"Nothing, 'Ami.' I hope that isn't a secret nickname that only 'Cami' is allowed to use. Funny, since *I've* known you since forever but never got a nickname."

Amethyst didn't even turn toward Rose. "I guess *Cami* is a better friend to me than you ever were."

It would've hurt less if Amethyst had shoved Rose off her seat and out a window. Chamomile Mills a better friend than *her?* Thoughts clanged through Rose's mind too quickly to process. Too quickly to even register how fast Amethyst was breathing or the broken shards of pencil she'd tried to subtly stuff in her backpack.

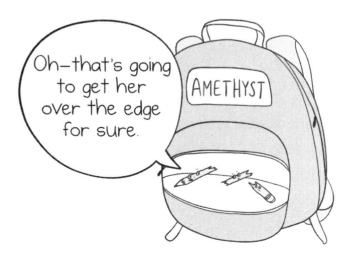

Chapter 27
AMETHYST

I should've turned her in, Amethyst thought as she went back to ignoring Rose's existence. *I should've washed my hands of all this. It's taking up too much brain space.*

Even now Amethyst was thinking of her fight with Rose instead of listening to Ms. Rainwater—not that anyone could really hear above the nonstop squawking of Hugo's plant. He'd brought his flower to class as a power move, to show he was going into his Check-in ahead of everyone else. But Amethyst wasn't intimidated. Not even a little bit. Never mind that her socks were nearly see-through with sweat. Or that she hadn't gotten a flower to even grunt, let alone sing.

Amethyst couldn't afford to be fazed. The Blossom Award would be hers, no matter what she had to do to get it. *Kind of like how Rose was willing to do whatever it took not to go to*—NO. Amethyst shut down the unwanted thought like popping a bubble. She and Rose were *nothing* alike. This was a completely different situation.

She reached for something else to focus on and landed

on the breakfast date she'd had with her mom that morning. And the sideways looks her mother had given Amethyst when she'd again stayed quiet during most of their meal.

"I'm glad we could catch up, just the two of us," Ms. Vern had told her. Without Julie and Sage, Amethyst had felt like she was under a spotlight. She didn't like the feeling.

"I hope classes are going well." Her mom speared at her quiche as she spoke. "You're such a smart girl, Amethyst. I know you're going to do great things in the world."

Amethyst had taken a long chug of orange juice, but when she didn't reply, her mom's eyes had shifted to her and lingered there.

She knew her mom missed nothing. It's what made her so good at her job keeping the peace with the Under City. Once, when Amethyst had been looking at her mom's new business cards with the pretty embossed little birds in the corner, she'd asked why the Firm's logo was a hummingbird. Her mom had said, "Hummingbirds are messengers. That's why they flap their wings so fast and seem to hover. They're listening."

"What if they don't hear anything?"

"Even better," her mother had said with a smile. "Silence can bring the most information."

There sure had been a lot of silence between Amethyst

and her mom lately. Enough for Amethyst to question if she'd ever be the smart girl her mom wanted her to be. The Blossom Award had once felt within reach; graduating with honors and getting a job at the Firm, too. But not lately. Not for a while now. Maybe she just wasn't good enough. Maybe she never had been.

"Ms. Rainwater?" Hugo purred, his hand flinging into the air. "Can we get extra credit if our flower sings in other languages?"

Something broke inside Amethyst. *My mother is going to realize I'm a failure*, she thought. She closed her eyes and shut out the classroom, the noise, even the sound of her breathing.

I wish I were anywhere else. Amethyst needed an escape, and she needed it now. Her mind wandered to the way the sunlight filtered in through her dorm room window, to Rose laughing on her floor and fresh notebooks scattered on her desk, to the assembly and how her ex–best friend had gone rigid as she stared straight ahead.

"Please," Amethyst whispered. She wasn't sure who she was begging. She just knew she couldn't let the tears fall, and wished her body would just vanish before anyone saw them. *"PLEASE,"* Amethyst repeated desperately.

Abruptly, with a strong gust of wind, the usual classroom smell of cinnamon was replaced by sea salt and something else. Something sweet and floral. A breeze brushed her cheeks and made the ends of her hair dance. When she opened her eyes, she thought she spotted a familiar figure in the very unfamiliar place. A place she'd never seen before. It was full of chalky white sand and crashing waves that angrily pelted against the coast. A field of beautiful, fragrant purple flowers stretched into the distance as the wind violently battered them.

"Lavender," Amethyst murmured into the gust.

The figure turned his head, as if she'd called his name. It was Lav Barros. But where were they? And how did they get here?

Amethyst's heart began to race. As she squinted into the harsh sunlight, a scratching sound filled her ears. The sound of someone roughly sliding their chair against marble floor.

Amethyst jerked awake, though she hadn't been sleeping. She was positive she'd been somewhere and seen something impossible. Her head whipped around the classroom, searching for Lav.

He wasn't there.

Breathe, she commanded herself, her heart vibrating. *BREATHE.*

Strained, Amethyst glanced around. Everything looked as it had been. Ms. Rainwater was writing the order the class would have their Check-ins on the board, and her classmates were dutifully listening. Everyone except Rose, who stared at her like she'd sprouted wings and was about to fly away. Something had happened—the look on Rose's face confirmed it. Amethyst had . . . well, she wasn't sure what she'd done, which sent panic shooting down her veins. But Lav might.

For the first time in her life, Amethyst wished class would end early. Every word Ms. Rainwater said seemed to bounce off her like a rubber ball. When her name was called to come up to Ms. Rainwater's desk for her Check-in, Amethyst couldn't even remember what she'd prepared to say.

"So, Amethyst, how is the assignment coming along?" Ms. Rainwater asked, hand poised over her grade book.

"Fine," Amethyst squeaked. She registered Ms. Rainwater's surprise at her one-word response. When it came to school, Amethyst usually had a lot to say.

"Have you run into any issues? Anything you want to talk through?" Ms. Rainwater leaned closer, as if trying to gauge what had upset Amethyst. Amethyst hoped the distant expression she wore wasn't too noticeable.

"No issues. I'm doing great." Amethyst's heel tapped restlessly, the ocean spray still clinging to her hair.

Ms. Rainwater's eyebrows knit in concern. "Are you sure, Amethyst? You seem distracted lately. Especially right now."

"Magic has my full attention," Amethyst said, looking Ms. Rainwater right in the eye. She wasn't exaggerating. Amethyst just needed to spout something believable so she could leave and track down Lav. "I've tried many different formulas with various flower species. I know I'm getting close. I'll have flowers singing in no time."

"All right, then. You're free to go," Ms. Rainwater murmured as she called the next student to her desk.

Amethyst grabbed her backpack and rushed out the door, too distracted to notice the sand coating her socks or that she'd almost barreled straight into Rose. In the hall, Jax and Felix narrowly missed getting clobbered. They leapt out of the way with just seconds to spare.

Amethyst left a trail of sand as she raced to get answers.

Chapter 28
ROSE

For a moment Rose forgot why she was standing in front of the class. The spot on her shoulder where Amethyst had slammed into her seemed to burn.

"Is everything okay?" Ms. Rainwater looked up from her desk and turned to a new sheet in her notebook.

Rose felt jumpy, her throat going dry with the memory of what she'd just seen. The air felt so thick, she worried it wouldn't even go to her lungs, instead sinking into her knees and weighing down her whole body.

She half registered someone calling her name. "Rose? Rose?"

"Yes?" Rose squeaked out.

"Are you going to sit?" Ms. Rainwater asked, brow arched.

Rose dropped into the vacant seat across from her teacher but fought the urge to glance over her shoulder. There was no point. Amethyst was long gone by now.

Rose wasn't sure what she'd seen. But she was positive she'd seen . . . something. It had looked like Amethyst had faded, as if her light had dimmed. She hadn't been translucent exactly, just not quite solid. It'd been too subtle to notice unless you knew Amethyst's hair wasn't just black, it was onyx, and her skin wasn't just brownish tan, it was a burnt sienna that glowed from within. But Rose noticed. And it terrified her.

Amethyst was in trouble. Accidental-magic-in-the-middle-of-class trouble. And Rose didn't know how to help. The last thing she cared about was the Equinox Test. Rose wasn't willing to waste her energy on non-Amethyst things right now.

She rushed Ms. Rainwater through the Check-in, admitting she'd been having some trouble but promising to double down on research and spell practice. By the time she was dismissed, Rose wondered if the path she was walking led straight to Rogers Middle. If her dismissive attitude and the empty pages of her notebook doomed her in an irreversible way.

But her best friend needed her. Everything else would have to wait.

Chapter 29
LAV

Lav wanted to make good on his promise to Rose. He'd meant to come clean ages ago but had kept making up excuses: He needed to study, the dishes needed to be done, his sneakers could use a cleaning. The distractions from his conscience were endless.

Until one rainy Tuesday morning, when one less guilt-leaf on the guilt-tree in the guilt-forest sounded too good to pass up. He'd walked into Principal Ivy's office before he lost his nerve.

"Uh . . . h-hello . . . I mean . . . hi." Lav stumbled over his words as he walked through the open door. He hadn't planned any further than his greeting.

"Hello, Lav." Principal Ivy rested her elbows on the desk. "Glad to see you in school this morning." She raised her eyebrow at him.

Lav dipped his head, not ready to talk about his absences just yet. He was here to confess to the cheating, not every wrong he'd ever done. As he started to slump into the chair across from her, a violent hiss filled his ears.

Sitting on the seat, as if *they'd* been in a meeting with Principal Ivy, were Jax and Felix. Their tails fluffed up as they sprung from the seat, both sashaying through the door and into the hallway without a second glance.

"Oh, um, sorry." Lav wasn't sure why he felt the need to apologize, but he had the feeling he'd interrupted something.

"It's fine. They'll return once we're done. Please, take a seat." She pointed to the chair across from her. Lav sat.

"Ivebeenmeaningto—" Lav cleared his throat, his nerves jumbling his words together. "I need to talk to you. To come forward about the Equinox Test and, um . . ."

Lav sat on his thrumming hands. He could do this.

"I'm the one who cheated." His voice was low, almost a whisper. "I tried to get answers for the Equinox Test from a friend, but I couldn't even really hear what she was saying, so it wasn't much of an advantage, and then I was inter-rupted . . ." Lav trailed off. He didn't want his rambling to throw Rose under the bus.

Principal Ivy took a long deep breath before she spoke. "You're a good student, Lav. You weren't going to have any trouble on the Equinox Test. Making flowers sing is well within your capabilities. Why cheat?"

Lav looked up and met her gaze. She didn't seem mad, just curious. Curious and disappointed.

"I didn't know that getting that kind of help wasn't allowed." Lav hated the way his eyes felt, like someone had sprinkled salt in them. "It's my fault. I took some bad advice. I thought that finding out what was on the test would give me the same advantage my classmates had." It was the honest truth, even if it sounded ridiculous. "I guess I didn't want to believe it was cheating."

"I understand." Principal Ivy nodded. "I just wish you had come talk to me, or really anyone you trust, about what you were feeling."

Trust wasn't something Lav did easily.

"I'm sorry," he said, and meant it. "I know I'm probably expelled—"

"You're not expelled." Principal Ivy raised the corner of her lips. "You'll be taken out of consideration for the Blossom Award, and you will have to complete a different Equinox Test. But this is still your school."

A soft "thank you" was all Lav could manage.

"Taking responsibility for your mistakes is a good lesson to learn young," Principal Ivy replied.

Lav couldn't believe his luck. Confessing had gone much better than he ever thought it could.

Principal Ivy gave him a long, hard stare. "I will, however, need to talk to your parents."

That brought Lav back to reality. Explaining things to Principal Ivy was one thing, explaining to his parents was another. Lav wasn't ready to do that just yet.

"With the language barrier, it's probably better if it comes from me," Lav reasoned. He'd exaggerated his accent just a little. The principal didn't need to know that both his parents spoke English.

Principal Ivy gave him a long look. Her eyes said she wasn't buying it, but her mouth said, "I'm sure your parents would really appreciate hearing your side of this story."

That sounded to Lav like she wasn't going to call them. Two wins from one meeting was more than anyone could ask for, so he quickly stood to leave. Lav looked down at his pants, which were covered in cat hair.

"Why are the cats even allowed in the school?" Lav growled with some frustration as he tried to wipe the fur off. He preferred dogs. Cats were too sneaky.

"Felix and Jax work for the school. They keep an eye on

things." Principal Ivy smiled as she spoke. "Felix was patrolling the corridor when you went into the Correspondence Room."

Patrolling? That sounded very official for a school pet . . .

"I got snitched on by a cat?" Lav couldn't believe it. He'd never trust those furballs again.

Principal Ivy raised her palms. "As I said, they keep an eye on things." She grabbed a folder from her desk, clearly getting back to work and dismissing him. "So now you know some inside information your classmates don't."

As Lav left the office, he was smiling.

Chapter 30
ROSE

Rose walked to school early the next morning and waited on the lawn outside Amethyst's dorm until her former best friend emerged from her room.

She knew she'd never get Amethyst to talk about what happened until she wasn't so angry. So Rose would do the only thing she could: make apologizing to Amethyst her full-time occupation.

Only nothing she said seemed to matter.

"Amethyst, please! I'm sorry, okay? You have to believe

ROSE VERA

Professional Apologizer

me," Rose pleaded as she followed Amethyst to the cafeteria for breakfast. "Hasn't this gone on long enough? I miss you. We both said things we didn't mean."

She was met with silence in the egg line, silence at the juice bar, and silence at the long, cold dining table.

Rose sighed. Since when was she the mature one? "I saw what happened in class, you know. What's going on with you?"

Amethyst just rose, her scrambled eggs half-eaten. Rose watched from the table as Amethyst took her tray and trotted back to her room.

No matter, they had a day full of classes together.

In each one, Rose enchanted a secret note to the inside of Amethyst's textbook that jumped from page to page as she read.

Please talk to me.—Rose

I've said sorry a thousand times. I didn't mean any of it.—Rose

Why won't you believe me?—Rose

Aren't you at least impressed by this magic? I'm not usually good at stuff like this!—Rose

But Amethyst ignored them.

Rose had never channeled so much concentration into her magic before, and the strength of the spells kind of overwhelmed her. Had she really had this power inside her all along?

Amethyst didn't respond to anything Rose did, which only made Rose try harder. Rose couldn't give up. What if the next time Amethyst half disappeared, she didn't come back? Or worse, what if she fully disappeared?

"Why do you care so much?" Lav asked Rose after school. They were sitting on Butter Crust's roof picking squash for the Harvest Festival. Rose hadn't seen him at school in a while and was surprised to find him at the restaurant when she showed up with her dad. Not missing a beat, Rose filled him in on all he'd missed but left out the part about Amethyst's accidental magic. Rose wouldn't go spreading rumors about Amethyst, not even to Lav.

"I'm just worried about her," Rose said evasively. "She works herself too hard. And I'm ready to make up."

"But you two aren't even friends anymore." Lav said it casually, as if Rose and Amethyst never speaking again was actually an option.

Rose stood and put her hands on her hips. "Clearly, you've never had a best friend." She turned on her heel, ready to walk home, rest up, and do it all again tomorrow.

Chapter 31
LAV

That weekend Lav followed his mom around the maze of stalls at the Harvest Festival, his arms full of sunflower-yellow corn and bloodred radishes. The festival was crowded, as usual. Kids dashed from booth to booth for maple sweets and apple slices, while their parents huddled together whispering about the previous night's earthquake, their faces concerned. Lav had felt it—every cell in his body had shuddered all at once. He'd asked his parents about it that morning, but his mom said she'd assumed it was just the nearby train. Had it actually been an earthquake? Lav wasn't sure.

He also wasn't sure why the entire Magical Community had nothing better to do on a Saturday morning. Lav bit back a sigh. Heads nodded toward him and his parents as they walked through the marketplace. He even recognized a few teachers from school.

Lav hoped none of them came over to say hello. He hadn't been to class in days, not that his parents knew that. But as he looked around at the stocked stalls of jewel-toned vegetables and fragrant fruits, he realized a lot of students had probably been absent. Harvest season meant all hands on deck.

The sound of steel drums floated through the crowd, and Lav let a grin escape. Though he still wasn't a fan of the festival, he appreciated the smell of grilled lamb and onions that always hung in the air. His mom added a fistful of carrots to his pile and Lav's arms quivered under the weight. He knew he should've brought the cart, but he'd been too distracted as they'd left their apartment.

A thought kept tugging on his brain and wouldn't let go: He'd seen Amethyst in a place she shouldn't have been.

Lately, Lav spent most of his time Shifting to Île Violette. He still went to school, but instead of attending class, he'd find a quiet, hidden spot to camp out for the day. The Brooklyn School of Magic had no shortage of good hiding spots.

Sometimes he'd meet up with his grandmother, and sometimes he'd just spend the day staring out at the water alone, his thoughts crashing into him like waves on the shore.

But one day last week as he sat lost in the sand, he'd nearly jumped out of his skin when Amethyst of all people had called his name. Or had he imagined the whole thing? There was no way she'd come looking for him, much less know how to get there. At least, he didn't think so.

It seemed his thoughts had summoned her, because as he rounded a corner, the Butter Crust tent in sight, Lav was greeted by an exasperated shriek.

"WHERE HAVE YOU BEEN?" Amethyst screamed at him. She seemed to realize how loud she was when Lav's mom turned toward them and arched her eyebrow, a smile playing at her lips. Soon Lav's parents ambled away, giving him privacy for whatever Amethyst was about to unleash.

"Where have you been?" Amethyst whispered.

"What do you mean?" Lav replied. He was grateful his parents were out of earshot. If Amethyst really had been at that beach, he was glad they weren't around to hear about it. They didn't exactly know about his . . . trips.

"You haven't been in class all week," Amethyst seemed to pant. "But I saw you. I saw you . . . Where were we? How did I—?"

"*Oh.*" Understanding softened shoulders Lav hadn't even realized he'd been tensing. "I guess you really were there. Did you Shift by accident?" He took a few tentative steps away from the crowds toward the tomato stall.

"Is that what that was?" Amethyst wore a frustrated look, like she was mad at herself for not realizing she'd Shifted sooner.

Lav knew Shifting could be a reaction to stress, which was probably what happened to Amethyst. She was lucky— Shifting was dangerous for inexperienced Magic Bearers. It left a trail of bread crumbs, but some people never found their way back to their bodies.

"But—why were *you* there?" Her words were sharp, accusing.

"Okay, Officer, simmer down." Lav bristled, adjusting the vegetables in his arms. They were starting to get kind of heavy. Lav didn't owe Amethyst an explanation, but he also didn't need her telling everybody what he'd been doing when he wasn't in class. "I meet my grandma there sometimes. It's cheaper than airfare."

Lav was more homesick for Île Violette than ever. Sure, the island had its problems. But maybe if his family had stuck it out longer, things would've gotten better. A wistful part of him hoped that when his parents found out about the cheating, they'd see that he was becoming someone desperate in Brooklyn, someone who made bad choices, and would send him home because of it.

"Your grandma was there?" Amethyst reached over and grabbed the radishes from his full arms.

"No, not that day. She—" Lav's words fell from his lips as a withering stare caught his eye. Rose stood planted in the middle of the Butter Crust tent with her arms crossed, rage radiating from her as community members parted around her like the sea.

Amethyst followed his look and fidgeted uncomfortably, the radishes jostling in solidarity.

Rose started toward them like an angry cat, each prowling step meant to punish.

"Oh, hi, Lav," Rose said as she stared Amethyst in the eye.

I don't think she's really talking to me, Lav mused. It was probably best to stay out of whatever was about to go down. Soundlessly, he backed up a few steps and settled in a nearby folding chair.

Chapter 32
AMETHYST

To her credit, Amethyst didn't look away. She stared back at Rose with a defiance that was only slightly undermined by the way she was nervously biting her lip.

"Yes, Rose?" Amethyst said, all ice.

"Oh, so we're actually speaking?" Rose shook her head. "Good to know."

Amethyst didn't have the patience for this, not right now. She was still stuck on the fact that she'd Shifted, which was more advanced magic than she'd ever done before. The idea thrilled and scared her. Her mom Shifted sometimes for work, and had described it as a mental library—a way to store information that might be useful. And now that she'd done it, she could see that it was so much more. Being able to travel wherever and whenever you wanted . . . The possibilities felt endless to Amethyst. Maybe she could finally see the Under City, or even visit her mom's library. But could she Shift somewhere she had no idea how to get to?

Before Amethyst could think about what might be

possible, she had to deal with Rose. She turned and placed the radishes on a nearby table, her hands moving to her hips. "It's not like you gave me much of a choice." The apology notes Rose had sent her in class had been beyond frustrating, even if the magic was admirable. Amethyst always knew Rose could perform complicated magic if she applied herself. She just wished her ex–best friend would apply herself to something other than bothering her. Amethyst took a breath. She was in no mood to forgive anyone today. "Some of us are actually trying to pay attention in class, Rose."

The blow hit its target. Rose looked shocked for a second, then seemed ready to spew fire. But she hesitated, not immediately jumping down Amethyst's throat.

That's new, Amethyst realized. Rose wasn't normally someone who held back.

"If you had responded to any of those notes or even gave me a chance to speak, you would know I'm trying to help you." Rose's tone was clipped, but the earnestness in her voice caught Amethyst off guard.

Still, she didn't need help. Especially not from Rose. "Why would you think I need—"

"So you partially disappeared during class on purpose?" Rose shot back.

"I Shifted." Amethyst paused for effect, hoping the impressiveness of her feat would cover the wobble in her voice. But Rose noticed it, because of course she did. "Some of us don't need help, we have natural talent," Amethyst threw in.

She knew that was unkind. Unkind and untrue. But she didn't like the worry in Rose's eyes. She'd rather see anger or judgment there because if, even after everything, Rose sought her out knowing she'd be ignored and insulted, then they might still be best friends. And if they were still best friends, Amethyst would have to face things she didn't think she was brave enough to hear.

"Why'd you have to cheat?" The question burst from Amethyst's lips, an explosion that had been brewing for far too long. "How could you put me in that position? And Dawn, too. This stupid fight is all I've been able to think about! You know

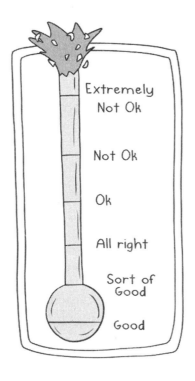

Extremely
Not Ok

Not Ok

Ok

All right

Sort of
Good

Good

how much my mom expects from me. If I don't win the Blossom Award, she'll be so disappointed. And how could you say she—" Amethyst hadn't meant for her voice to break.

How could you say my mom didn't want me? Amethyst couldn't bring herself to repeat the words out loud. Her small suspicion that it was true had been growing day after day, though this was the first time she'd let that feeling take shape. The stinging in her eyes was predictable enough, the trail of tears along with it.

"I WASN'T THE ONE WHO CHEATED!" Rose shot back. "It was HIM!" Her finger pointed at Lav's chest like a weapon. "He cheated, not me."

Lav shot Rose a hurt look. "Why'd you have to drag me into it?"

"Oh, be quiet," Rose snapped. "It's too late for that now."

A few heads had turned in their direction, but no one seemed to be listening. Of course they didn't—there was food to be eaten and news to be shared. *For everyone but the three of us apparently*, Amethyst thought as Lav stood. Quickly gathering up his produce, he nodded his head toward the path and started walking. This was not a conversation to have in public.

Amethyst was wet-faced and in a state of genuine shock as

the girls followed Lav away from prying eyes. Once they were tucked behind a shady tree a few tents down from the Butter Crust stall, whatever trance Amethyst had been in vanished.

"You cheated?" She threw the words at Lav, who wouldn't meet her gaze. "But I was so sure . . ."

If what they said was true, it wasn't Rose who was the problem, it was Amethyst. *She* was the one ruining her *own* life. Killing her shot at the Blossom Award. Keeping her mom from being proud of her. Sabotaging her future and the chance her mom would ever trust her enough to join the Firm one day. If I'd just believed Rose from the start, if I'd been brave enough to ask Dawn—

"I can't deal with any of this right now!" Amethyst turned on her heel and sprinted.

It had finally happened. Amethyst had reached her limit.

Chapter 33
LAV

"Thanks a lot," Lav sneered at Rose. "I asked for your help, not to tell the whole world my private business."

"Amethyst needs our help more right now," Rose snapped. "So maybe stop obsessing over yourself for five minutes and help me look for her."

She marched down the street, leaving Lav blinking with his arms full of vegetables. He spotted his parents nearby and rushed to them, glad his dad had finally found a bag to put their stuff in. Lav dumped the bounty inside, his arms feeling like noodles.

"I, uh, have to help a friend." Is that what Rose was? His friend? "I shouldn't be long."

His dad smiled. "Go ahead, we'll see you at home."

Lav raced to catch up to Rose, who was heading for the school a few blocks away.

"Wait up!" he called, then jogged until they were side by side. He'd never seen Rose so anxious. Maybe he should distract her a little to take the edge off while they searched.

"Did you really mean what you said earlier? That I obsess over myself."

"Absolutely," Rose said, a little too quickly. "You think people are thinking about you way more than they actually are. Everyone has their own stuff going on. Nobody cares if you say 'hamburger' a little differently."

He still said hamburger differently? He'd thought he'd fixed that.

"Well, sorry not everyone can be as bold and uncaring as you, Rose," Lav shot back as the school came into view.

"I care a lot. But about things that *actually* matter. Like Amethyst." Rose's steps pounded the sidewalk. "Not useless things like other people's opinions."

"You're unbelievable," Lav muttered.

"*I'm* unbelievable? You're trying to distract me while I search for my best friend! She Shifted by accident during class the other day, did you know that? Do you know how dangerous that could have been?"

"Yeah, I know she did . . . because I was at the place she Shifted to," Lav added.

"YOU WHAT?" Rose paused, then kept walking. "Why were *you* there? How'd you even do that?"

He was not in the mood to get blamed for Amethyst's

accidental magic. "Do you even know how Shifting works?"

"I do," Rose continued as they went up the front steps. "My brother actually taught me how to Heart Lead, which is even more advanced than Shifting, thank you very much. Everyone I love is connected to me and I don't need some preplanned dream destination to find them."

At the front door, Rose paused, looking for a sign that Amethyst had been there. "Where would Amethyst go?" Lav asked, trying to be helpful. "Maybe she's in her dorm room?"

"No." Rose shook her head. "I think she's upset because this whole time she thought I was the one who cheated. Knowing her, she went looking for answers."

"Why did Amethyst assume it was you?"

"Because I told her I was going to cheat." Rose didn't sound even a little bit bothered by it. "And I went to the Correspondence Room to do exactly that. I was going to get in touch with Dawn, Amethyst's cousin."

Rose's eyes lit up. Then she turned toward the Specialty Magic wing and raced toward the Correspondence Room.

"Dawn!" she called over her shoulder to Lav. "She's going to find Dawn!"

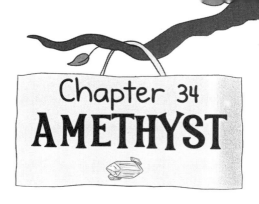

Chapter 34
AMETHYST

It was the weekend, so the school was nearly empty. Amethyst stalked through the halls without really seeing, fury following her like a close friend. Somehow, her feet led her to the Correspondence Room.

She grabbed a Communication Portal from its stand. It was lighter than she expected. She knew she wasn't supposed to be in here using it without a teacher present, but rules would have to wait until her world felt more stable.

She followed the vague instructions she remembered reading once, her hands slick on the Portal's wooden frame. "Dawn," Amethyst begged, "take me to Dawn." The frame began to shake, but nothing happened. Was it broken? She glanced around for a manual, but all she could see was a thick maple door with *Dawn* printed in rolling letters on a small plaque.

The door abruptly swung open, and the scent of smoldering palo santo drifted from her cousin's tidy desk. From

the way Dawn's eyes scanned the hall as she poked her head out, it seemed like she was expecting someone else.

"What are you doing here?" Dawn's eyebrows rose as she glanced down the hallway again. "Come in, come in."

She ushered Amethyst inside, her fingers swiping air where Amethyst's shoulder should've been. It was like Amethyst was made of smoke.

"Where'd you find a Communication Portal?" Dawn asked as Amethyst stood near the small bed pushed against the wall.

Amethyst really needed to start answering some of these questions, but she didn't know where to start.

"Did she really not do it?" The words spilled out of her like a full cup of water sloshing on a bumpy tray.

"Who—?"

"Rose. She didn't do it?" Amethyst couldn't hide the plea in her voice.

"Oh, this is about Rose!" Dawn said, her head tipping to the side. "Did she really not do what?"

Amethyst fixated on Dawn's confusion. As if Dawn had expected her to be talking about herself. Had news of Amethyst's meltdown reached the university before she could even explain herself? She'd barged into her cousin's room unannounced and was ruining everything. She always ruined *everything*.

"Hey, don't read into it." Dawn went to reach for Amethyst even though she wasn't really there. "I just meant that in last night's Committee meeting, one of your teachers mentioned that you and Rose weren't speaking. Did something happen?"

"She CHEATED!" Amethyst spewed, her eyes closing against the moisture that began to build. "She did! Or, um, she almost did. Rose meant to—with you! On the Equinox Test!"

Dawn seemed to understand and smiled sympathetically at her cousin. "She never contacted me. To my knowledge at least, Rose did not cheat. But don't beat yourself up over it, Amethyst. I'm sure—"

Amethyst's eyes snapped open. "I ruined *everything* because of this! Did Principal Ivy even do a proper investigation?" Amethyst wrung her hands, her eyes blinking quickly. She'd already risked too much to be wrong about this.

"Wait." Amethyst's words moved before her mind could catch up. "Why was I mentioned at a Committee meeting?"

Sure, the fight had been world-ending for Amethyst. But

why would all the leaders of the Magic Bearer Community care if she and Rose weren't speaking?

Dawn bit her lip. It sent ice down Amethyst's spine. The spinning wheel of her mind began to slow for the first time in months. Something was wrong . . . and it had to do with her.

"What's going on?" Amethyst's eyes were as clear and still as twin lakes.

"It's nothing." Dawn ran her hand through her short hair and looked down at her feet. "Nothing you should be concerned with, Amethyst, anyway. At least not yet."

Yet? The word clanged around Amethyst's skull.

"You should let this go. This fight with Rose isn't worth your energy." Dawn leveled a look at Amethyst, as if soon she would need all the extra energy she could get.

Amethyst considered her cousin's words, her heart starting to race. "How much can you tell me?" Amethyst began, her voice small.

"I really shouldn't . . ." Dawn huffed a breath. "Isn't there a student at the school from Île Violette? Lavender, I think? He was on the island when the trouble started, before anyone realized it would come for us all. Did he tell you what it was like? Has he warned you?"

Amethyst opened her mouth and closed it, adjusting her

glasses as her eyebrows furrowed. *Lav and Île Violette? What trouble? What does Dawn mean?* Had Amethyst allowed her world to shrink to the size of a pinprick, not letting anything else matter besides her personal drama? Amethyst glanced at the worry etched on Dawn's face. Amethyst had a feeling she wouldn't have the luxury of her world being that small again.

She reached for the part of herself that was like her mom—the part that missed nothing. She'd allowed a misunderstanding to obscure everything else going on in the world. But no more.

"I'm sorry," she whispered. "I don't know anything about Île Violette. Not really." Then she clamped her lips shut so nothing else could escape. She needed answers, but her cousin had already let slip more than the Committee would tolerate, and she knew she'd have to look for them somewhere else.

Amethyst flinched as someone cleared their throat, so surprised she dropped the Communication Portal. Dawn seemed to reach for her through the frame, but before Amethyst could say anything more, Dawn and her dorm vanished like sand on the wind.

As the Correspondence Room came back into view, Principal Ivy cleared her throat again.

Now that she was looking for them, Amethyst saw the stress lines on Principal Ivy's face, making Amethyst wonder just how bad things were. Her lips tilted down ever so slightly, and her eyes looked heavier than they had even just a few weeks ago, as if she'd been up all night.

Thanks to Dawn's warning, Amethyst wasn't surprised by Principal Ivy's quiet worry. But she was surprised to see Rose and Lav standing behind her. They must have followed her. Rose's concern was clear as she scanned Amethyst to make sure she was okay. Lav just looked happy to be relieved of his corn and radishes.

But how much did he know about whatever had happened on Île Violette? From the relaxed way he leaned against the wall, probably not much. They needed to talk, all three of them. Soon.

They'd wasted enough time skirting around things. It was time to clear the air and own up to their actions—whether they were proud of them or not. But first, Amethyst needed answers.

"Follow me," Principal Ivy said, as if reading her mind.

As Amethyst followed, she was grateful Rose was by her side.

Chapter 35
AMETHYST

"Lav was the one who cheated," Amethyst blurted out when they were alone. Principal Ivy had asked Rose and Lav to wait in the hall.

"I'm aware of what happened. Mr. Barros and I have already discussed it. I've brought you here to discuss something else." Principal Ivy's tone was short. Her lip trembled slightly, betraying the tidal wave of emotions that crashed underneath her cool exterior. "Last night, your mom was found in possession of a wand."

The words knocked the wind out of Amethyst. Her mother would never, ever—

"An investigation is underway, and you and your sisters are going to spend winter break with the Vera family. We've already contacted them and have arranged to have your things moved when it's time."

This was a mistake. Amethyst was certain of that. She'd just had breakfast with her mom the other day.

"You shouldn't have to answer questions about your

mother and who or what she's gotten involved with." Principal Ivy's discomfort spread like a strong wind, and once it hit Amethyst, her foot began to bounce with anticipation. "But, sadly, shielding you from those questions isn't a luxury we have right now." Principal Ivy sighed. "What do you know about Heather Vera?"

A very dangerous wand, not to be confused with Lav's long-lost great stick.

Chapter 36
LAV

"Stop eavesdropping," Lav scolded. "It's not polite."

"Neither is cheating," Rose muttered, her ear pressed shamelessly against the door. "I think she just said 'Heather.'"

Lav gave her a judging raise of his eyebrows, and Rose snorted, as if she didn't care what he thought.

"Do you think she means the flower or a person?" Rose leaned farther in. "I have a cousin named Heather."

"I know a Heather, too." Lav shrugged. "The world has a lot of Heathers."

"My Heather's in Chicago." They could only make out muffled murmurs now, so Rose switched tactics, squatting to the floor to see if she could hear better from the small crack below the door.

"The Heather I know is from Chicago, too . . ." Lav watched Rose straighten. *There's no way—*"

"South Side, on Prairie Avenue?"

"With the park across the street?" Lav's voice was nearly silent.

Heathers are great!

"Green eyes?" they said simultaneously.

"That's my cousin." Rose took a step back, eyeing Lav suspiciously.

"Of course she is." Lav dropped his head. His family had gone to Chicago for a few weeks over the summer to see his dad's friend Jared. The twelve-hour drive, which his mom insisted on for the "scenery," had been brutal, and the late July air had been muggy and thick. Lav was used to heat. Île Violette had been hot, but Chicago in the summer was a different kind of heat. Lazy and sluggish from the perpetual blaze of sun on asphalt, Lav had vowed to never set foot in Chicago again. He'd spent most of the trip sitting in a puddle of sweat in front of the fan.

They'd gone sightseeing downtown and around Hyde Park, and on the second week, visited a man his dad had been corresponding with for years. It was at Jared's cozy South Side bungalow that Lav had met Heather, Jared's daughter, and apparently, Rose's cousin.

She was sixteen, had finished Middle Magic, and was about to begin Specialty Magic at the Chicago Academy of Magical Arts, where her dad was the dean.

What's a "dean"? Lav had wondered at the time. The way Heather described it, a dean was similar to a principal. *They do things differently in Chicago,* Lav realized.

Heather had been nice enough, but seemed on edge during their brief conversation. She'd kept asking him questions about Île Violette and had seemed disappointed by his answers. The island was his home, and he loved its sun and sand—what else had she been expecting to hear? He didn't want to talk about the tensions there or his family's move, so he switched the conversation to school. She'd scrunched her nose when he mentioned Mr. Kneely and how much he'd liked his Charms class. Talking to Heather was exhausting.

"If you ever need help, let me know," she'd blurted once Lav had run out of polite things to say. "Especially with the Equinox Test. Seriously, call me. Everyone gets the answers from their parents anyway, and as a dean, my dad has access to every magical curriculum in the country. Even Brooklyn's."

The casual way Heather had said it, like it was no big deal, put Lav at ease even if he wasn't completely sure Heather could be trusted. She'd told him about the Communication Portals and where to find them, shocked that he didn't have his own. According to her, everyone else did. *Typical*, Lav had thought.

He figured that since her dad was in charge of the Chicago school, Heather might be a valuable resource and a good friend to have. Maybe he'd judged her too quickly. She was being very generous with her knowledge after all. Hugo called things like this "networking."

Not that she'd actually been much help. The Communication Portal transported him to a place covered with fog and winds so harsh they snatched every word she'd said. It'd been a miracle he'd even heard her say "singing." Just the memory of it made Lav bristle.

So why had she been willing to risk so much for a stranger? If they'd been caught, they both would have had to pay a hefty price. Lav wasn't sure what Heather was up to, but he didn't like it.

"I think your cousin set me up." Lav turned to Rose, her

eyes so different from the emerald green of her cousin's. "Why would she do that? She doesn't even know me."

Rose shook her head. "That's Heather."

"Well, I'm not keeping any secrets for her," Lav spit out. He felt used and frustrated. "I'm telling Principal Ivy it was Heather I talked to on the Communication Portal the minute she's done with Amethyst."

He'd expected Rose to bristle—this was her cousin he was turning in after all. But she'd leaned against the door in thought.

"Heather . . ." Her mouth worked as if trying to find the right words. "She's had a hard time since she lost her mom a few years ago. So she acts out."

Lav hadn't known that. "But why did I have to get caught up in her little game?"

"Maybe she wanted you to tell on her from the start. Or maybe she didn't think you'd actually follow through on her offer." Rose shrugged.

"But her dad's a dean. She has to know that giving someone the answers to the Equinox Test would've gotten her expelled."

Rose seemed to mull this over. "Maybe she wants to get expelled."

"So she could do what? Have all the time in the world to ruin other people's lives?" Lav slumped to the floor. How long were they supposed to wait in this hallway anyway? Could they go back to the Harvest Festival?

"Heather's not evil." Rose's voice finally became defensive. "She can just be impulsive. You had your reasons for believing that what you were doing wasn't wrong. Maybe she has her own reasons, too. This situation is tangled and messy, but she's not a bad person. Really."

The difference was that when Lav realized he had broken the rules, he'd felt terrible. *Does Heather regret what she's done?* Lav wondered. *Does she know about all the chaos she's brought to Brooklyn?*

Chapter 37
AMETHYST

This was all just a mistake, thought Amethyst. *It has to be.*

Her mom was going to come to the Blossom Ceremony, where Amethyst would win the award, and then she and her sisters were going back to New Jersey to enjoy a restful winter break. That was the plan, and that's what would happen.

But what if it doesn't? a small voice inside her squeaked. What if her mom really *did* have a wand and really *had* disappeared? Amethyst had felt that strange sensation last night, like her bones were shivering. Had everyone felt it? Was it because of the wand? What would happen to Amethyst and her sisters? And what did it have to do with Rose's cousin?

"Heather has been missing for two days," Principal Ivy explained. "The last known person she was in contact with was your mother. And I'm sorry to have to tell you this, but as of last night, your mom has now disappeared as well."

"No!" Amethyst choked out as all the air drained from her lungs and all the blood rushed from her brain. She was breaking apart cell by cell. One more word and Amethyst would be nothing but mist.

I can't be here. The thought was like a lightning strike. *I can't do this. I have to get out of here. Go somewhere else,* Amethyst commanded herself, eyes squeezing shut. *NOW!*

The wind that swept Amethyst up was familiar—she'd felt it in class the other day. She was Shifting again. It felt like a tornado swallowing her whole, the air denser and more solid than it had been before.

And as the wind knocked her glasses to the floor, Amethyst vanished.

Chapter 38
ROSE

On the other side of the office door, Rose heard a shout. She didn't hesitate, yanking it open just in time to see Amethyst's vacant chair topple, her gemstone-red glasses clattering to the ground.

Horror painted Principal Ivy's face. There were a thousand spells Amethyst could've just done, and every single one of them was far too advanced for Elementary Magic. Rose knew Amethyst was really upset, and in that state, she could hurt herself.

As Rose's hands became slicked with sweat, Principal Ivy grabbed a folder that read CODE RED PROCEDURES. In a flash, vines shot from the floor to their respective destinations, alerting the Committee and calling for help. Then Principal Ivy began muttering tracking spells. Her frown told Rose they were coming back empty.

"This is the last thing we need—" Principal Ivy was mid-thought as Rose, a wild look in her eye, picked up the ruby-red glasses she'd helped Amethyst choose back in their second year. Amethyst couldn't see without them. Her whole world became a blurry watercolor painting. She was somewhere upset, alone, AND unable to see? What if she'd transported herself somewhere dangerous? *No. No, no, no.* Rose wouldn't let anything happen to Amethyst.

Reed had said Heart Leading was only for emergencies. And if your best friend disappearing wasn't an emergency, then what was? Rose tried to remember everything Reed had taught her.

With Shifting, only a person's essence transported. Those special bits that made you *you* left your body, but the rest of you stayed behind as an anchor. Amethyst was gone. All of her.

This was very powerful magic, and Amethyst might not be able to find the bread crumbs that would lead her back. What if she was lost forever?

No. Amethyst being lost forever was unacceptable. Someone would have to go and get her. And, apparently, that someone would have to be Rose.

Lead with your heart. Reed's words echoed in her head. That was the difference between Shifting and Heart Leading. For Shifting, your head decided and everything else followed. To Heart Lead, Rose would have to let her heart entirely guide the way, trusting that it would lead her to her friend.

It wasn't until she'd already cleared her mind and focused her breathing that it occurred to Rose her heart's compass might be a little rusty after the fight she'd had with Amethyst. They'd exchanged a lot of hurtful words, and even if her brain did her best to forget them, Rose doubted her heart had. Going after Amethyst this way might be speeding down a collapsed bridge. Reed had been very specific. Both the Traveler and the Receiver had to feel the connection between them. Otherwise, they'd never find each other.

Suddenly, Rose felt her mind and heart tugging her toward something warm and spacious. Her eyes flung open in alarm. Could she really do this?

Principal Ivy's shout never reached Rose. She was already gone by then.

Rose hurtled through violet skies past a tornado of wind and light, her mind pushing the doubt away as everything she loved about Amethyst rose to the surface: her quiet resilience, how kind a sister she was to Julie and Sage, the stable and consistent presence she'd always been in Rose's life, how she gave anyone a chance, the way she found nothing impossible and was always one plan away from taking over the world. The more Rose focused on Amethyst, the more her fears melted away from her heart.

She was tossed in a whirlwind of leaves and petals, dirt and soil, their energy spreading a prickly magic through her veins like warm honey.

"I'm coming, Amethyst!" Rose felt herself reaching out, her heart straining. "You're not in this alone!"

But was she strong enough? Was she really good enough at Magic Bearing to find her friend?

She landed with a thud. Chest heaving, she peeled her head from the soft, powdery surface and fought to catch her breath. Her heart pounded in her chest like it was trying to escape her ribs, which were sore and achy. Rose hadn't known magic could take this much out of a person.

She looked up, and the ocean's surface twinkled back at her in greeting. Outlined against the shore, the small silhouette of a girl with long onyx hair floated in the breeze.

Chapter 39
AMETHYST

Amethyst dug her toes into the warm sand. Maybe she could stay here forever, just leave New York and all her worries behind.

You can't do that to Julie and Sage, her brain scolded. How was she going to explain this to her little sisters? Their mom was suspected of having a wand and was being blamed for Heather's disappearance—as if Heather couldn't get into trouble all on her own. And now Amethyst was left to deal with this mess. She couldn't even get flowers to sing for an Elementary Magic test; how could she be capable of handling all this?

When Rose appeared beside her, Amethyst's eyes went wide. She was too tired to be angry. "What are you doing here?"

"I couldn't let you have *all* the fun." Rose lay back on her elbows as if she was on a beach vacation.

"How'd you find me?" Amethyst asked.

"Reed taught me to Heart Lead a while ago," Rose said

casually. "I know you think I'm not good at magic but—"

"I never thought that. I always knew you could do anything you wanted to." Amethyst held Rose's gaze for a second before looking away.

"Where even are we?" Rose looked around, her eyes paused on the endless rows of lavender.

"Île Violette, or some form of it, I think." Amethyst grabbed fistfuls of sand. "It's where I came last time. Maybe this is the only place I can go." She stared out at the ocean as if all the answers were just underneath its surface. The tide seemed to roll up to greet her in answer, the water reaching out to her. She sensed it was reluctant as it ebbed away.

"I'm sorry, Amethyst. Really, you have no idea how sorry I am." They both looked out at the horizon as Rose spoke. "I let my fear of ending up at Rogers Middle ruin everything. If that's where I'm meant to be, then that's where I'll be. End of story."

"Rose, you just Heart Led." Amethyst almost smiled at her familiar tone of voice. It sounded like the old her, the pre-fight, pre-Principal-Ivy's-office Amethyst. "They're not going to send you to Rogers Middle, not after you just did magic way harder than making flowers sing."

"Why do you think that is?" Rose looked genuinely

confused. "Why can't I figure out something that should be simple? The spells for those notes I sent you were so tricky. I don't know why I can do the advanced things but not the basics. I couldn't even get my flowers to whistle." Rose shook her head.

"Neither could I." Amethyst shrugged. "I didn't think I'd have any trouble this year academically and I'm barely getting by. My magic must be getting weaker." Amethyst looked down at her hands.

"Amethyst, you just did a Shift so powerful your body disappeared. Most *adults* can't even do that." Rose nudged Amethyst in the ribs. "I saw you boil water like it was nothing with my own two eyes, and now here you are, summoning the ocean."

The thought stirred something in Amethyst.

"You know how magic with water comes so naturally to me? Well, maybe complicated stuff comes naturally to you." Amethyst could believe that. Rose was smart. Lack of ability had never been her problem. Boredom was. Apparently, the complicated stuff could hold Rose's attention.

They sat in silence, the ocean waves pushing softly against the shore, so different from the harsh crashing Amethyst had seen last time.

"I didn't mean all that stuff I said to you," Rose forced out. "I just wanted to hurt you in that moment. I don't believe for one second that your mom doesn't want you." Rose waved her arms as she spoke. "I don't know what's going on with this wand business and whatever else, but your mom loves you. No matter what."

Tears fell silently from Amethyst's eyes, and her voice wobbled. "I'm sorry for what I said, too." She leaned her head on Rose's shoulder, and Rose wrapped her arm around her. "I let our fight get way bigger than it should have been."

"Can we be best friends again?" Rose whispered.

"I don't think we ever really stopped," Amethyst said with a wet laugh.

She wasn't sure how long they sat together, the warm sand cradling them as a lavender-scented ocean breeze played in her hair. Even if there was a mile-long list of problems waiting for Amethyst in Brooklyn, she didn't have to handle them alone.

She and Rose would face the unknown together.

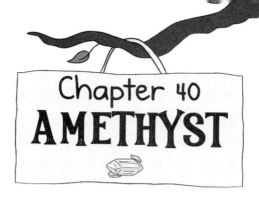

Chapter 40
AMETHYST

Amethyst wasn't quite sure how she and Rose got back to Principal Ivy's office. One minute Rose was handing back her glasses and telling her not to worry, and the next she was surrounded by worried faces. She felt groggy. Less solid than she was used to. But she pushed all that aside and concentrated on the only thing that mattered: her mother.

Even if she made a mistake, she's still my mom.

For the rest of the afternoon, Committee members filtered in and out of the office, asking question after question about Amethyst's mom. Rose stayed by her side. Amethyst answered what she could and took a lot of breaks. She didn't know much about her mom's work or the Firm, only that what had once seemed glamorous now reeked of suspicion. And so did the big project in the Under City her mother had been occupied with over the last few months. Had she really been keeping the peace, or were there other secrets under the surface, hidden deep where Land Walkers and their magic were forbidden to go? A headache was lodging itself right behind Amethyst's eyes.

Lav stuck around for a while, explaining how he'd met Heather and what he'd seen through the Communication Portal. Amethyst had lots of questions for him about Île Violette, but now wasn't the time.

As the day went on, it became clear that last night, when Amethyst's mom had gotten a wand and disappeared without a trace, she hadn't Shifted. To truly leave no signs meant she'd used very powerful magic. Nature *always* left a trail behind. But her mom had shattered the trail, and wherever she was she didn't want to be followed. Magic like that shouldn't have been possible.

That meant that whatever her mother was involved with, the magic she was using was powerful enough to have killed the ancient tree the wand came from. The entire grove could have even been wiped out. The grave faces of the adults said as much. And the entire Magical Community would have to face the consequences. If last night's tremor was any indication, it had already begun. Nature would have no choice but to take something in return. If her mom still had magic, Amethyst doubted she'd keep it much longer.

And then there was the true wild card in all this: Heather,

who had also gone missing. According to Principal Ivy, when Rose's uncle had searched for clues to her whereabouts, he'd found a small white business card with a hummingbird embossed on the upper right corner in her bedroom. Ms. Vern's business card.

No matter what, she's still my mom. The chant was constant in Amethyst's head.

By the time Julie and Sage were summoned to Principal Ivy's office, Amethyst was drained. They looked so small, surrounded by grown-ups with serious faces. Somewhere out there, their mom was in trouble. The thought haunted Amethyst, but she didn't want that for Julie and Sage.

"Hey," Amethyst chirped, squatting down so she could be at their eye level. She plastered on a smile she didn't have the energy for. "Everything's all right, it's just . . . Mom went away for a little bit."

"Where?" Julie's eyes scanned the room.

"Why?" Sage's lip began to tremble.

Amethyst should've asked to talk to her sisters alone.

"I don't have all the answers, but . . . everything's fine. *We're* fine. We're going to spend winter break with Rose and her family. We'll eat cookies and make snow angels; it'll be fun. Mom will be back soon." No one in the room believed her. "Mr. Bear can even come. We'll have a special pillow just for him."

"And a little blanket, too," Rose added, offering Amethyst a small smile of encouragement.

Julie and Sage nodded, but the fear in their eyes still troubled Amethyst.

A few Committee members questioned the girls, but they knew even less than Amethyst. Whatever was going on, Ms. Vern hadn't involved her daughters.

As they finished up in the office, Amethyst wanted nothing more than to lie face-first in bed for a few weeks.

"Are you sure you don't want to sleep over?" Rose asked as people began filing out the door, Lav offering a wave as he went. "Seriously, come to my house. I'll ask my dad to make pancakes in the morning. Julie and Sage can come, too!"

"We're going to be together all winter break." She'd given Rose the same response the other four times she'd asked. "I just want to be alone for a little bit."

The walk back to the dorms was slow, each step heavy, as if bricks had replaced her feet. She deposited her sisters at their rooms downstairs and trudged to her own, her mind still racing from the day's events. That morning the biggest issues in her life had been her fight with Rose and the

Equinox Test. Now she knew she'd been lucky to have those be her only problems.

When she finally crawled into bed, Felix relinquished her lumpy, cat-hair-covered pillow and nestled against her feet. She was grateful for his comforting presence. But the more she tried to sleep, the more her brain insisted on keeping her awake.

Mom left us. Again.

Amethyst's eyes stung at the thought. All day she'd craved some space to think with no one watching, but now, alone in the dark, thinking was the last thing she wanted to do.

Maybe I should've had a sleepover with Rose after all . . .

A soft knock on her door interrupted the thought. Was it Principal Ivy coming with more bad news? When she slowly opened it, there were Julie and Sage, pillows in hand.

"Can we stay in here tonight?" Sage asked.

Amethyst exhaled. She hadn't truly appreciated how close her dorm was to her sisters' until now.

"Of course." She opened the door wider, her shoulders relaxing. They piled all the pillows and blankets Amethyst had on the floor and made a giant fort. Even Felix joined the snuggle fest, making himself right at home on Mr. Bear's chest.

Julie and Sage fell asleep almost immediately, their chests rising and falling with each breath. As Amethyst settled in beside them, her dreams pulled her away like a current. In the dream, water swirled and waves crashed all around her. Kyle the koi fish swam by in a topaz-colored current, a rush of bubbles following him as Lav, waving a radish and eating a quiche, chased after him. Awake or asleep, Amethyst couldn't seem to escape the Under City.

Chapter 41
LAV

After the Harvest Festival, Lav expected Amethyst's mom to be a big topic of conversation—which she was. It seemed like everyone was speculating about what might have happened. Even the koi fish were whispering about it.

A week later, the incident continued to cast a long gray shadow over the school. Soon the sun was dipping lower in the sky and cloudy days were outnumbering sunny ones. Lav felt sorry for Amethyst. He knew it wasn't fun to be a topic of conversation.

So far, though, she'd taken it like a champ. Lav usually

I heard that she charmed herself into a butterfly and flew away.

saw her in the library with Rose, reading in the gardens with her sisters, and of course at lunch, which they all ate together now. Chamomile Mills had even joined them a few times.

Lav wasn't sure how it had happened, but somewhere in all this mess, he, Amethyst, and Rose had become friends. It was a gravitational pull he couldn't fight. Suddenly they were all in one another's orbits. Amethyst put on a brave face, especially when her sisters were around. Still, he was glad he could be there for her even if all he could give was his company.

Their teachers seemed to be giving everyone a break. Even they seemed shaken up. Lav hoped the school might even cancel the Equinox Test with everything going on, but his hopes were quickly shattered.

"No, the test is not canceled. It will be conducted tomorrow as planned," Principal Ivy said when they ran into each other as Lav headed to Charms class. Had she read his mind? And where had she even come from? With a thorough scan of the hall, she continued on her way before Lav even had a chance to reply.

He woke up the next day to gloomy skies and the kind of breeze that required a sweater.

Test day, Lav considered as he brushed his teeth. He didn't even know what his test would be. He was supposed to be given a new assignment because of the cheating. But after everything that happened with Amethyst's mom, it seemed like he and his new test had been forgotten—which he was more than okay with.

It bothered him that his parents still didn't know about what he'd done. It bothered him a lot. Lav put down his toothbrush and splashed water on his face. It was time to confess.

Lav walked out of the bathroom, ready to face his destiny, only to find his parents sitting at the kitchen table waiting for him. He couldn't tell if their expressions were grim or nervous.

"What's wrong?" Lav's heart skipped a beat. "Did something happen to Grandma?"

"No, no, nothing like that." His dad shook his head as Lav took his usual seat between his parents. "We've got some news, Lav, it's—"

"Wait," Lav interrupted, his mouth moving before his mind could catch up. "I have something to tell you first." He looked at his parents, his mom's wavy brown hair clipped back in a long braid and his dad's eyebrows mirror images of his own. *This is not going to be fun.* Lav took a breath and began.

He'd only meant to tell them about the cheating. But with their faces open and eyes gleaming, he just couldn't stop talking. All his feelings tumbled out of him—how sorry he was to shame their family name, how embarrassed he felt that he'd let them down, how desperate he was to adapt to the way things were done here more quickly, how much he wished he was worthy of all they'd given up. And how no matter how hard he tried, he just wasn't.

"So I'll go back to Île Violette." His voice shook with the salty tears carving into his face; he didn't dare look up from the tattered place mat his eyes were glued to. "I'll go live with Grandma. Or maybe we can all go back together." His voice broke again. "That way you guys don't have to keep working so hard to give me opportunities I keep wasting." He looked up as hands pulled him out of his chair and wrapped themselves around his trembling shoulders. His dad smelled like za'atar and aftershave. Lav felt his mother's gentle embrace join them.

They stood like that for a long time. Long enough that when they broke apart, the wet patches on his cheeks had mostly dried, even if new tears were still running down his mom's and dad's faces.

"Why didn't you tell us how you were feeling?" His

dad held him at arm's length and gripped his shoulders protectively.

"I didn't know how to." His parents already lived with exhaustion from working so many jobs. He didn't want to make their days harder by complaining or seeming ungrateful.

"Well, you're talking to us now. That's what matters." Mrs. Barros wiped her face and sat back down at the table, clutching Lav's hand and drawing him to her. "When Principal Ivy called, I told her you were a good boy. That you'd come to us yourself and tell us what happened."

"You knew this whole time?"

His mom only shrugged.

"So I can go back to the island?" Lav sounded almost hopeful as he sat hand in hand with his parents. He'd never been so grateful for the tiny round table.

"No, Lav. None of us are going back." His dad gave him a light smile that was sad. "Île Violette just isn't safe for Land Walkers anymore. The tides are rising. The Merfolk's disagreements are having consequences for us all, not just in the Under City but everywhere. And now, with a wand in the mix . . . Soon, there might not be an Île Violette to go back to."

"What about Grandma?" They couldn't just leave her with nowhere to go.

His parents shared a look. "Grandma is already waiting at our new house," said his mother. "In Chicago."

"Chicago?" The word clanged through Lav's head, erasing everything else. He was barely settled in Brooklyn and they were already moving again?

"I've been taking night classes these last few years, getting my teaching certification." Mr. Barros's dimples gleamed. Lav's mom nodded along. "And I haven't been just working at Butter Crust. I've been apprenticing. I oversee the health and maintenance of the restaurant's lake."

"He even introduced a new species of algae into the ecosystem," his mother added proudly. "The entire winter menu is being built around it, that's how delicious it is."

"I'm so sorry we didn't tell you about the move sooner." His dad closed his eyes, the movement heavy with regret. "Nothing was definite, and we wanted you to focus on school and friends, like all the other kids. Once I got my certificate, I applied to teach at the Chicago Academy of Magical Arts."

"They have the best aquatic program in the world," Mrs. Barros declared, triumph in her eyes.

"And you got the job?" Lav jumped to his feet and tackled his dad in a bear hug.

"You're looking at the Chicago Academy's Head of Seaside Horticulture!" The joy radiating from his dad thawed something deep inside Lav's heart.

"And while your father was taking classes, I've been experimenting with hybrid seeds. I'm hoping to open my own seed shop in Chicago. Grandma has even scoped out a few storefronts for me." Mrs. Barros took Lav's face in her hands. "My love, we took this leap and moved to New York for you, yes, but we did it for ourselves, too." She leaned in to kiss his cheek. "Our love isn't something you need to earn. Not ever. I'm sorry we didn't do a better job of explaining that."

"So we're definitely moving." Lav dropped into his seat, not expecting the small pang in his chest. He had people in Brooklyn, Lav realized. People he would be leaving behind.

"Your dad's position wasn't supposed to start until fall. But since the dean's daughter disappeared, the school asked if we could come early so your father could take over some of his courses." Mrs. Barros sighed. "My heart breaks for Jared Vera. He is living a parent's worst nightmare."

"When do we leave?" Lav's voice sounded tentative as he

looked around their one-bedroom apartment. Some of their things were already in boxes.

"Just before winter break." His dad gave him a sympathetic look. "You'll start at the Academy in the spring."

A new city. A new school. A familiar shiver sped up Lav's spine. *A new home.*

Lav saw the excitement in his parents' eyes. They were so eager for all that awaited them. It made this move feel different. They weren't running away from something. His parents were following their dreams. And his grandmother was joining them.

Maybe now, as the guilt-forest that had surrounded him seemed to dissolve and the guilt-trees shrank back into guilt-seeds, Lav could finally let himself figure out what *his* dreams were.

Maybe he'd even start introducing himself as Lavender.

Chapter 42
ROSE

The day of the Equinox Test had finally arrived, and Rose was worried. She got to school early, ready to accept her fate at Rogers Middle. Regardless of what Amethyst had said on the beach, Rose couldn't make a flower sing. She wasn't going to pass.

She tried to savor her steps as she walked through the school because they felt numbered. Maybe she should go find Amethyst, who was probably eating breakfast by now. As Rose considered her next move, she noticed a green smudge snaking along the corridor.

Rose stopped walking. The green smudge stopped, too. She started walking again, and it followed. She sprinted down the hall, along the river, and over the footbridge to a small meadow in the Elementary Magic wing. *Some water would be so nice right now*, Rose thought as she tried to catch her breath.

Elbows resting on her knees, Rose felt a cool nudge on her shoulder. She turned and found an ice-cold glass of water

wrapped securely in a green vine dotted with ivy leaves.

"Thanks," Rose muttered. It was suspicious, but she was definitely thirsty, so she took the glass.

The vine seemed to bob its head as she drained it. *This must be the smudge*, Rose realized. It had been following her.

As if in answer, the vine grew to Rose's height, an ivy leaf stretching to the size of a plate right in front of her eyes.

Please report to Principal Ivy's office was printed across the leaf in gleaming gold letters.

The awesomeness of getting a vine message quickly faded as Rose registered its meaning. *They're not even going to let me try to take the Equinox Test, huh?* She knew she wasn't going to pass, but they at least could've pretended she had a chance.

Five minutes later, Rose sat, once again, across from Principal Ivy. *I should get this seat engraved with my name*, she thought as she hung her head in defeat.

"Miss Vera." Principal Ivy sounded like she was glad to see Rose and slid an envelope across her desk. "Congratulations."

Rose was confused. For a moment she just held the envelope, her thumb softly tracing the school's emblem on the milky-white paper. Once sense returned to her, she tore it open, nearly shredding the neatly folded paper inside.

Dear Miss Rose Vera,

Upon examination of the extraordinary magic you exhibited mastery of in tracking and returning with Miss Amethyst Vern, we proudly invite you to continue on to intermediate coursework, also known as Middle Magic.
You are hereby excused from the Equinox Test.

Sincerely,
The Committee

Pride, relief, triumph, and a million other feelings swirled inside Rose like a rainbow. Hundreds of words bubbled to her mouth, but somehow the ones to break through were "TAKE THAT, ROGERS MIDDLE!"

Waving her letter like a flag, she left Principal Ivy's office and sprinted across the footbridge and the moss-covered riverbank to Redwood Dorm, then up the stairs because she couldn't be bothered to wait for the elevator, and right to Amethyst's door.

Amethyst opened it with a grin, her own letter in hand with a similar message inside.

"Middle Magic is lucky to have us," Rose declared,

dragging Amethyst into a hug. They'd really done it. Despite everything, they had accomplished what just a few months ago had felt impossible—they were going to Middle Magic. Together.

Rose nearly floated to Ms. Rainwater's room to watch her classmates take the test and cheer them on like the mature almost–Middle Magic pupil that she was. As each student was called to present, their flowers released a high-pitched sound like a violin. Rose wasn't sure they were actually singing, but she applauded the effort all the same. Each plant's sound was distinctive but familiar, like remembering a face she hadn't seen in a while.

"Hey, Cami," Rose whispered. "How *do* you get flowers to sing?"

"You ask them what they have to say," Chamomile responded. Her daisy's high-pitched soprano had somehow sounded soothing rather than earsplitting.

"That never even occurred to me. I just kept trying to force them." Rose's eyebrows knit in recollection.

"We all did. It wasn't until Mr. Sol's lecture on tulips that I even realized how alive plants really are, with their own histories and everything." Cami smiled. "Once I started listening, they had a lot to say."

"Talking to flowers is pretty impressive." Rose would have to give this listening-to-plants thing a try.

"Not as impressive as Heart Leading," Cami said, eyes as wide as saucers.

Chamomile Mills might not be so bad, Rose decided as Magnolia brought her daffodils to the front of the class.

As lessons ended and students flooded the hallway, Rose searched for Lav in the crowd. He hadn't presented a flower, and she wanted to know why. Amethyst and Rose had both performed complex magic, but all Lav had done was watch them.

"What do you mean you didn't have to take the test?" Rose gasped once she and Amethyst finally cornered him.

"I'm moving," said Lav. "To Chicago."

"So you're just automatically in Middle Magic at the Academy?" Rose raised an eyebrow. To think, all this time she could've just moved to the Midwest.

"At the Academy, they take the test during the first year of Middle Magic, not the last year of Elementary." He shrugged, a new lightness in his eyes that Rose hadn't seen before. "I have another semester to study."

"I'm actually going to Chicago over winter break," said Rose as they walked toward the arboretum for the Blossom

Ceremony. "Amethyst, too. So you won't have to miss us too much."

Lav rolled his eyes, but she could've sworn relief flooded his face first. He would miss them. She was sure of it.

"We're staying with my uncle," Rose continued. "The two of us, my parents, Sage, Julie—the whole gang."

"Won't that be . . . complicated?" Lav turned to Amethyst. "You and your sisters staying there while your mom is linked to Heather's disappearance?"

Amethyst hesitated, then shrugged as she turned into the South Arboretum. "Principal Ivy said it doesn't look like Heather put up a fight or anything. Maybe she left on her own. Either way, my sisters and I didn't have anything to do with it."

The trio took their seats. Rose spotted Sage and Julie with their classmates a few rows ahead of them.

"We don't have to talk about that right now." Rose shot Lav a stop-asking-hard-questions look. "We just need to focus on the Blossom Award and celebrating that we got through the Equinox Test. The hard part is over."

"Or it's just beginning," Lav said under his breath.

Rose elbowed him in the ribs.

Chapter 43
AMETHYST

As seats began to fill up, Amethyst spotted Rose's parents and Reed sitting next to Mr. and Mrs. Barros. The lights dimmed and everyone took their seats as Principal Ivy came onto the stage.

"Welcome to the Brooklyn School of Magic," she began to thunderous applause. "It is my honor to welcome you to this year's Blossom Ceremony."

They all knew Hugo would get the Blossom Award. Even though his yowling carnation had been more annoying than anything else, the tonal range had been impressive. Regardless, Amethyst involuntarily flinched as his name was called.

Sorry, Mom.

"Hugo made some petals whine, big deal," Rose huffed to Amethyst in solidarity with what she clearly considered a snub. "You performed a Shift that made you completely vanish without even trying. There are people in Specialty Magic who can't even do that." Rose clapped exactly two times for

Hugo as he walked to get his award, then crossed her arms.

"Give Hugo a break," Amethyst whispered with a laugh. He was one of very few people who hadn't been whispering about her these last few days. "He earned it."

"This year, I'm pleased to announce we will also be awarding the Medal of Excellence in Magical Achievement," Principal Ivy continued.

Amethyst sat up in her seat, eyebrows raised. The school rarely gave out the Medal of Excellence. Not even Dawn had gotten it. And if Dawn wasn't excellent, then who was? But she had a pretty good idea of who it could be and grinned so wide her face hurt.

"For her extraordinary command of Heart Leading under extremely stressful circumstances and her spirit of determination, I am so pleased to award this to Brooklyn's own Rose Vera." The applause for Hugo's award was like a kitten's meow compared to the lion's roar Rose received.

Rose walked toward the stage looking shocked. Her eyes locked with Amethyst's as if asking for permission to be happy about this.

Yes! Amethyst wanted to scream. She jumped to her feet and began to cheer. "You deserve this, Rose!"

A lightness filled Amethyst as Principal Ivy placed the medal around Rose's neck. The last few months had been tough. And she still had so many questions. Where had her mother gone? Why had she taken a wand? What did she want Amethyst to do? Yet here she was, still standing. And getting to cheer on her friend, who was finally being celebrated for the extraordinary person that she was. Even with the cloud of drama surrounding her, Amethyst was grateful to get to be here witnessing this.

Maybe it's okay that it isn't me, Amethyst thought amid the thunder of applause. *Maybe it's even better that it's Rose.*

She spotted Julie and Sage jumping up and down. Their smiles and laughter were contagious. Was this how her mom felt when she got to cheer them on? Was this why she pushed them so hard—not to simply win awards or be the best, but so they could be celebrated? So they could feel loved? Maybe that's all her mom had really ever wanted for them. For her.

I wish you could see this, Mom, Amethyst thought with a shaky breath. *I wish I could share this feeling with you.* Despite everything, Amethyst felt closer to her mom than she had in a long time.

As if in answer, Amethyst felt a tug beneath her ribs. Like someone had poked at her heart. When the applause quieted and Amethyst took her seat, her mind raced back to the beach on Île Violette. Rose had been rubbing her ribs, hadn't she? And when she'd grabbed Amethyst's hand to take her back, Amethyst had felt a duller version of that same sensation.

Mom . . .

Amethyst didn't know much about Heart Leading, let alone communicating with your heart, but there was no way it worked like this. Her mom couldn't be trying to communicate with her. It wasn't possible.

Was it?

Chapter 44
AMETHYST

Back home, after a celebratory lasagna dinner, Rose and Amethyst cozied onto the couch in the den.

"I'm full," Amethyst declared.

"Me too," Rose agreed. "Everything is as it should be. I'm not and never will be going to Rogers Middle, I have a shiny new medal I'm still not sure I deserve—though I did hang it on my wall with a little spotlight—and you're staying for a sleepover. We'll even get to hang out with Lav in Chicago for winter break. Life is good!"

Amethyst arched her brow. "Well, aside from my mom and your cousin vanishing, the all-powerful wand that's somewhere out there, and that dead patch of ancient magical trees."

"Those are tomorrow's problems," Rose casually dismissed.

Amethyst knew her friend was trying to comfort her, and she appreciated it. Tentatively, she slid Rose a look and bit her lip before clearing her throat.

"Hey, I've been meaning to ask you a question. How did

you do that magic in Principal Ivy's office?" Amethyst asked it casually, but her voice held an edge. After what she'd felt in the arboretum, she couldn't wait for answers to find her anymore—she had to find them.

"What do you mean?" Rose sank into the couch, letting out a contented sigh. Felix, who nestled on a nearby pillow, gave a satisfied stretch in response.

"How did you find me on the beach? I know we're connected to everyone we love. But how does that really work?" Amethyst's mom was trying to communicate with her, she was sure of it. And she needed to learn how to communicate back.

Before they'd left the school that evening, Amethyst had stopped by her dorm to grab some things. Alone in the safety of her room, she'd kneeled over the small pot of violets she kept on her windowsill.

"What do you have to say?" she'd asked, just as Cami had done. But nothing happened. It was disappointing to know she would've failed the Equinox Test. She'd felt like such a fraud for getting passed on to Middle Magic.

But Amethyst had glanced at the river as she rushed past it, eager to get back to her friends. White water lilies dotted the surface like little balls of light. During the day the water was clear blue, reminding Amethyst of the ocean in Île Violette. But at night it turned an inky black, its depths seeming endless.

"Well, what do you have to say?" Amethyst had grumbled at a water lily, not expecting an answer.

"What are you ready to hear?" a singsong voice soft as mist responded.

Amethyst stuttered to a stop. She'd done it! But the excitement was short-lived as she'd stared into the river's mirrored surface. An unnerving suspicion had taken hold of her.

She'd sprinted back to the arboretum, appearing at Rose's side panting and breathless. But she hadn't told anyone what happened. Amethyst needed to understand it herself first.

Why did it feel like as her magic got weaker on land, it got stronger in water?

Back in the Vera household, Rose glanced over her shoulder to see if anyone else was listening before answering Amethyst. "You mean Heart Leading?"

Amethyst thought of that mental library her mom had always Shifted to, hoping it held all the answers she thought it did. Was that where those heart tugs had come from? Was her mom leading her there?

Amethyst had been searching for answers, but maybe they'd been inside her this whole time. When she got back to school, she was going to have a long talk with that water lily.

But that was for later. Now she and Rose had important things to discuss.

"Yeah, Heart Leading," she said. "Can you teach it to me?"

Amethyst was ready to hear everything.

TO BE CONTINUED . . .

ACKNOWLEDGMENTS

Thank you forever to my amazing agent, Wendi, for your incredible guidance and support.

Thank you, Andrea Davis Pinkney, for believing in and championing this story before there was much to believe in.

Thank you to my incredible editor, Jenne, for your love and care for these characters and their journeys. I was really intimidated to do my first novel and I'm so grateful that I got to do it with you!

Thank you to my husband, Pat, for always being my biggest cheerleader. None of this could happen without you—you make life magical.

Thank you, Kristina, for our writing sessions at Panera and for being my very first author friend.

And thank you to Mom, Dad, the Honestys, and the Montagues for making New York and Chicago feel like extensions of home.

Love always,

Liz

ABOUT THE AUTHOR

Liz Montague began as a cartoonist for *The New Yorker* in 2019. She is the author-illustrator of the graphic novel *Maybe an Artist*, which was nominated for an NAACP Image Award; the picture book *Jackie Ormes Draws the Future*; and the middle grade series School for Unusual Magic. Liz is passionate about nature and emotional literacy. She lives in Philadelphia, PA, with her husband, Pat.